See what foll
Tom Deady's

"Tom Deady's *Weekend Getaway* demonstrates that his talent isn't limited to a single style. In the same way that his first novel, *Haven*, played a variation on a theme of early King, this short, shocking book is an extreme horror riff in the style of Brian Keene or Richard Laymon. Deady's out to show that he's no one note performer. *Weekend Getaway* does just that. Listen up! This cat can play.

– Bracken MacLeod, Bram Stoker Award nominated author of *Stranded* and *Come to Dust*

"Tom Deady's *Weekend Getaway* is a suspenseful thriller raring to dismantle the notion of the idyllic New England vacation. You won't be able to set it down."

–Glenn Rolfe, author of *Becoming* and *Blood and Rain*

"Unsettling as hell. Deady's tale will get under your skin and stay there."

–Ronald Malfi, author of *Bone White*

"There's a reason Tom Deady is already winning awards—he's a wonderful writer who's gonna make waves in this genre for a long time to come! With *Weekend Getaway*, Deady takes us on a nail-biting trip into the boonies with characters who are scarred, both physically and emotionally. When you're done with this one, you'll be damaged too."

–James Newman, author of *Animosity*, *Ugly as Sin*, and *Odd Man Out*

"Brutal and tense, this is one getaway you don't want to miss. My heart is still pounding."

–Hunter Shea, author of *We Are Always Watching*

"I flat out loved this book. It grabbed me and pulled me in, with brutal honesty, suspense, shock, and ultimately, peace. *Weekend Getaway* is easily the best book I've read in 2017, and perhaps for a couple of years before that."

– John R. Little, author of *The Memory Tree*, *Miranda*, and *Little by Little*

Weekend Getaway

Weekend Getaway

Tom Deady

Introduction
by
Josh Malerman

A
Grinning Skull Press
Publication

ISBN: 1-947227-02-5 (paperback)
ISBN-13: 978-1-947227-02-6 (paperback)
ISBN: 978-1-947227-03-3 (e-book)

DEDICATION

For everyone who ever believed in me…

CONTENTS

ACKNOWLEDGMENTS

Weekend Getaway is a shade or two darker than most of my stories, but I hope a bit of hope shines through. That was the intent.

First, I'd like to thank Michael Evans for giving *Weekend Getaway* a great home, and for turning this around in time for a Halloween release. It is greatly appreciated. Speaking of Grinning Skull Press, a round of applause for Jeffrey Kosh of Jeffrey Kosh Graphics for creating the eye-catching cover art. People *do* judge a book by its cover, and I'm thrilled to have such a beauty.

A very special thanks to Josh Malerman, author of *Bird Box, Black Mad Wheel,* and *Goblin*, and all-around cool guy. Not only did he agree to write the introduction, he knocked it out of the park. I'm forever grateful for his kind words and enthusiasm for my story.

Ben Eads, author of *Cracked Sky*, offered great insight to an early draft. His input was invaluable to the final product.

Linda Nagle, editor extraordinaire, gave *Weekend Getaway* the help and polish it needed to be released to the unsuspecting public. I am forever grateful for her keen eye.

For all the authors, local and otherwise, who have supported me over the years, thank you. You know who you are, and there are just too many to name. The horror genre is truly a family.

To my wife, Sheila, whose undying support and encouragement keeps me going; never stop believing.

And always, for Shannon and Alyssa.

INTRODUCTION

How do you like your horror?

You into funny? Brutal? Crazed? You dig the heart-thudding page-turning thrill show? Who doesn't, right? Or maybe, *maybe*, you'd rather savor the stuff, immerse yourself, fall so far into a story that you'll one day recall it all as a memory of your own life lived.

I'm into all this. All ways. Most of us are.

Tom Deady, he is, too. Only here, with *Weekend Getaway*, Tom is giving us what we really want when we say we want it all ways:

Tom Deady is giving us *horror.*

Brace yourself. Or don't. Approach this story in

1

whatever way will make your experience the biggest. Because it's all there on the page to be read, to be felt, to be lived. *Weekend Getaway* is as much a gulp of Jolt® Cola as it is a quick snap of a rubber band on the wrist. It's smart, small, and (undoubtedly) effective. One of the many pleasures herein is that, while we're led to believe the narrator, John Baxter, is telling his grandson the story as we hear it, we learn early on that actually he's not. He's telling the poor kid something else altogether while telling *us* the truth. That's some meta-action right there, for those keeping score. And Tom does it well. He hides the story we don't want to hear while giving us (in secret, in private, an audience of one) the one we do.

Tom gives us Grandpa's truth.

And Grandpa's truth is brutal.

There are a couple scenes in this story that I won't ever be able to pluck from my mind. I imagine myself, years from now, at a summer party, the sun is high, friends are there, drinking, laughing, and someone asks, "Josh, are you okay?" And I, lost in thought, snap back to reality, somewhat still shaken. "Why, yes, I'm okay. I was just thinking about…*Weekend Getaway*…"

You'll know what I mean when you see the cell. Or you'll start to know what I mean, anyway.

But this story isn't a shot of brutality, a mean book, by any stretch. Maybe that's what makes it so damn exciting: at its heart, *Weekend Getaway* is the story of how two people survive, as the husband recalls it shortly after burying his wife. It's also a brief meditation on anxiety, and how sometimes the only thing for anxiety to become is *rage*. The John Baxter near panic attack scenes are palpable, and readers are advised to take the very advice John once received himself: "Ride the wave, my therapist taught me, it eventually crashes and slowly ebbs away." That's serious anxiety acumen right there, for those keeping score. And Tom handles it this way throughout, until the moment when John perhaps supersedes his condition, even when Rachel tells him...

... nope, not gonna tell you any secrets.

You'll breathlessly unearth those on your own. But I will tell you that *Weekend Getaway* leaves you wanting more. Not more of the story itself, no no, Tom gives you everything you'll want and need with this one. But better than that you'll close this book wanting more *Tom Deady*.

So, without further ado…

Wait… One more thing before I turn it over. The cover art goes a long way with this one. Flip back to it for a second. See that amazing cabin? Those windows? Looks like an awesome place, doesn't it? Looks like a helluva place to rekindle some long-gone love magic, eh? Well, it *should* be, of course, but Tom doesn't let you make yourself too at home. Because he's giving us what we came here for, after all:

Fantastic horror.

And so now… go on… see for yourself…

And ignore that engine rumbling in the background. The sound of strangers closing in.

Creeping up on your romantic weekend getaway…

Josh Malerman
9/6/17
Michigan

CHAPTER ONE

Now

I tightened the noose around my neck, then yanked it off with a grunt. I had referred to neckties as nooses for as long as I could remember; anyone that had to wear one every day to work was slowly killing themselves. And here was I, like an old fool, trying to attach one to my own neck.

With a tired sigh, I tried again to make the knot. Finally, Mary came over and pushed my hands to my sides, and with a few deft movements, had it looking perfect.

"There you go, Dad." She smiled and gave me a

hug. "Mom always loved you in a tie, so you have to look nice for her this one last time." If there was ever an occasion that a tie was perfect for, it was a funeral.

She broke down then, after being my rock through the whole mess. I held her close while my own tears spilled. I was sure I'd be out of them by now, but they just kept coming. When she pulled away, her face held a determined smile.

"We should go. There'll be plenty of time for this later."

She was my rock again. I nodded, silently chastising myself. *I should be the strong one. She just lost her mother.*

* * *

The service was lovely, as funerals go. My wife was one of the good ones. After the priest said his final words at the grave, I remained there alone, shooing anyone away, including Mary, who tried to talk to me, to console me. I stared at the opening in the ground, wanting nothing more than to crawl in with my wife and let them cover me with dirt. I don't know how long I stayed like that, the never-ending tears dripping down my face, absently rubbing my ghost finger. *God, what I'd give for another day with her.*

Finally, I trudged back to the car. Everybody would be back at the house, eating and drinking and talking like nothing had happened. I hated the tradition. I just wanted to be alone. To think, or *not* to think, and to wonder why I wasn't the one to go first.

I drove home, listening to an oldies station, taking my time. The day was overcast—as if the sun didn't want to attend such a sad event—the sky heavy with rain. A perfect day for a funeral. I would have preferred pouring rain and gusting wind. An angry day, to match my mood.

The scene at the house was just what I expected. A lot of people laughing, everybody eating and holding either a beer or a glass of wine. A fucking party, minus one guest. I played my part as best I could, making the rounds, accepting condolences, sharing memories, always a glass of water in my hand. *Maybe just one drink today, something to take the edge off.* I stuck with water, though, as it wasn't a day to get sloppy.

As the afternoon wore on, people began drifting away. I guess they thought they'd put in the appropriate time and wanted to get back to their lives. Most of them I wouldn't see until the next death. I looked around at the mess, too overwhelmed to even think about cleaning. Instead, I tossed a dirty napkin on the coffee table and plopped onto the couch.

It was just Mary and her husband, Jeff, and their son, Nick. Jeff was a good guy, some sort of computer programmer. He made good money, but more importantly, treated my Mary like a queen. *What more could a dad ask for?*

Little Nick looked just like his dad; tall and thin for his age with a face that looked wise beyond his seven years. Mary started picking up in the kitchen, but I waved her off. "Leave it. Come sit with me for a while, I'm too tired to even watch you clean."

They spread out on the couches and chairs around me. Empty cups and bottles littered the room, along with half-empty plates of funeral food. I pushed some trash aside to make room for my water glass. I was with my family, what was left of it, anyway. We talked a while about the service, and a little while longer about some of the folks we hadn't seen in a while. Nick was getting antsy. It was a long day of being good for him, for any kid his age.

He climbed onto my lap and looked up at me. His eyes were so full of wonder and curiosity, so full of youth that it made my heart yearn for such innocence. I wondered when my own eyes had lost that. *You know when.* His little hand clasped my gnarled old-man hand and pulled it to his face. "Grampy, you never told me the story of how you lost your finger."

CHAPTER TWO

Then

I inched the car forward in the bumper-to-bumper traffic, silently cursing myself for not getting on the road earlier. I snuck a glance at my wife in the passenger seat, trying to gauge her mood, and held that glance when I saw the look of sadness on her face. A car horn startled me and I pulled up a few more feet, throwing my hands up in frustration at the car behind me. "Calm down, we're not going anywhere," I muttered.

Rachel sighed. She hated when I got irate behind the wheel. I once followed a car for miles after being cut off, only to find the driver was a harmless old lady who probably shouldn't have been on the road in the first place. Rachel was not impressed. *Bad traffic and road rage are not a good start to the save-my-marriage weekend.*

"Do you want to stop and grab a…an ice cream?"

Rachel was silent for a beat too long. "No, let's just gut it out, okay?"

When I'd first suggested the weekend getaway, she was hesitant. *She never wanted to come.* I'd known it all along, but had been hoping she would give the time away a chance. My anger faded to a hopeless res-ignation. *We lost our child, and we're going to lose each other.* I knew without any doubt it would send me on a downward spiral that I was unlikely to recover from. *Hell, I'm already circling the drain.* Our friends used to think we were the perfect couple. *We were the perfect couple, and we can be again.*

The traffic finally started moving when a sudden series of honks and angry shouts pulled me away from my disjointed thoughts. I glanced in the rearview mirror and saw a pick-up truck cutting recklessly through the slow-moving procession. "What a dick…"

The driver flashed his high beams and leaned on

his horn as he swerved into the right lane, passed a minivan, then cut back into the left lane directly behind me. The driver and passenger were whooping and laughing, flipping off the other drivers that were honking at them. I looked straight ahead and gripped the wheel tighter. My eyes darted to the mirror, hoping the truck would continue its mad attempt to get through the traffic, but it had come to a standstill once again. The pick-up's windshield was tinted, and I couldn't see what the men looked like. But I felt them. Watching.

The traffic crept along and the pick-up stayed behind us. I ran my fingers through my hair, then wiped my dry lips with the back of my hand. We were trapped in a sea of cars with nowhere to go. Sweat dripped down my back and I squeezed the wheel tighter. My throat was dry and I felt the too-familiar panic building. "Sure you're not up for that ice cream?" My voice sounded shaky and I wondered if Rachel noticed. I felt her looking at me and knew that she did.

"You okay?" She sounded genuinely concerned.

I ran my fingers through my hair again, anything to keep my mind off my rapid heartbeat. And the truck. "Yeah, just the traffic, makes me edgy, you know?" But she *didn't* know. Panic attacks were something she had never suffered and didn't understand. The truth was, I'd never had them either until I started drinking too much. Then I learned the terror of feeling like you're either dying or going crazy, and experiencing the helpless humiliation that goes with it. The shame of having someone see you have one, and the fear that you might have another. Anticipatory anxiety, my therapist called it.

We held a memorial service for...the baby. The panic attack I had that day was debilitating. I remember running from the church, screaming that I was dying. I don't remember much else.

"What the heck, summer is for ice cream, right? Isn't there a little place up here on the right?" Rachel pointed towards a plaza up at the next light.

Relief crashed over me, drawing the panic back out to sea with it. Something else, something about the way Rachel had relented and even sounded happy to do it. A dangerous hope filled my heart. "Boston driving skills coming up." I threw on my blinker and edged my way into the right lane. In a few minutes, we were approaching the small strip mall that did indeed have an ice cream shop, along with some honky-tonk looking t-shirt shops and a tattoo parlor. I felt the best I'd felt since the trip had started.

Movement to the left caught my eye. The pick-up truck had pulled up next to us. There was room in its lane for it to pull up further, but it sat idling next to us, rumbling.

It was all pimped out for off-roading. Giant knobby tires, and a lift kit that made me crane my neck to look at the passenger window. Windows tinted dark, *illegally* dark, most likely. The gleaming black paint was pristine, telling me the truck likely never left the road despite the tricked-out appearance. Something was written in script on the passenger door, but the glare from the street lights reflected in a way that made it impossible to read. I reached the entrance to the plaza and started to turn in. The truck revved its engine and tore away in a cloud of burning rubber and the roar of a V-8. I could read the single word on the truck's door as it pulled away. *Badass*.

* * *

The ice cream shop, Sundae School, was packed, but I was happy to be out of the car. My heart rate and breathing were almost normal again. I looked around the shop with amusement. True to its name, it was a mash-up of every classroom I had ever set foot in. There were old-fashioned maps on some walls, blackboards on others. Posters of different literary classics covered the remaining wall space, and flash cards with math problems lined the chair rail. The mahogany counter was made to look like a teacher's desk, and the offerings had cutesy names like "Perfect Day for a Banana Split" and "One if by Land" for a single scoop and "Two if by Sea" for a double.

The clientele ranged from families to teenagers to elderly folks and everything in between. Some pop hit by a singer of indeterminable gender played in the background, but the hum and chatter of the customers drowned it out. Rachel and I stood in line looking at the menu, giggling at the funny names and deciding what to order. The line moved slowly, but I didn't care. We were getting along, and incredibly, we were enjoying each other's company. *This is us, this is how we used to be.* We reached the front of the line and placed our order. When our ice cream was ready, we lucked out and found a small table available. We stayed and talked for a good half hour after the ice cream was gone. I was laughing at something Rachel said when I happened to glance out the window. My laughter died. I wiped the back of my hand along my mouth.

The black pick-up truck was out there.

Its lights were dark and it appeared empty, though it was impossible to be sure with the tinted windows. I looked around the shop, trying to pick out the guys from the truck. Rachel was saying something, but all I heard was the rushing of blood in my ears and the screaming thought echoing in my head: *They're following me.* A moment ago, the shop had been filled with the sounds of kids laughing and teenagers flirting. Happy sounds. Now, everywhere I looked, I felt a hostile stare in return. People seemed to be eyeing me over their ice cream cones or quickly glancing away when I looked at them. A couple of guys in stained t-shirts and John Deere caps were staring at me and whispering. Another guy in his twenties stood against the wall with his arms crossed, just looking around. He wasn't in line or eating ice cream. *I have to get out of here!*

I jumped to my feet, my thighs hitting the table and sending the empty dishes crashing to the floor. Apart from the sound of breaking glass, the shop went quiet, making my clumsiness more obvious. Now, everyone was staring. I was already heading for the exit when Rachel asked me what was wrong. I crashed through the door, but the night air did nothing to help me catch my breath. Rachel put her arm around me and guided me toward the car. A blaring car horn made me cry out. *It's them!* I broke away from my wife and ran to the car.

I was leaning against the car with both hands on the hood by the time she caught up to me.

"You look like a cop just told you to assume the position. Want me to frisk you?"

If I hadn't been in the throes of a panic attack, I would have enjoyed her playful comment. Instead, I shook my head as if she had asked me a serious question.

"Give me the keys. I'll drive the rest of the way, okay?"

She sounds annoyed. I reached into my pocket and handed her the keys. *Too much of a pussy to even take your wife on a romantic getaway.* The door to Sundae School slammed closed and my head jerked in that direction, eyes wide. It was just a young couple with their two kids. I took long, slow breaths, trying to regain control as I slid into the passenger seat. I felt Rachel's gaze on me, but couldn't look at her. As my anxiety lessened, my humiliation rose. An ugly see-saw ride. I slouched against the passenger door and stared out the side window.

"Hey. It's okay, John. Keep breathing slow, in through your nose, fill your diaphragm so your belly sticks out, then exhale."

I felt like crying. I hated being a passenger. Driving helped me feel like I was in control. "Thanks, Rach."

She pulled back out onto the main road while I struggled for something to say. *How did she know to help me with my breathing? She's never done that before.* Traffic had thinned out a bit, helping to calm me down. "Thanks for helping out back there." It sounded weak, even to my own ears. *Why can't I say something tender? Or at least clever?*

Rachel started to say something, but stopped. She

stared intently at the road ahead, gripping the wheel to the point that her knuckles turned white. "I did some reading on anxiety and panic attacks."

I sat mute, staring at my wife. I realized what this meant. At least what it *could* mean. "Thank you. It means a lot. These things…it's so stupid—"

"No!" She braked at a red light and turned to me. Her eyes were bright, intense. "Don't beat yourself up, okay?"

A horn blared behind us. The light was green. I turned to scowl at the car behind us. It was the pickup truck, right on our tail. Rachel accelerated with the road open in front of her, but the truck stayed locked on our bumper. Rachel's eyes flicked towards the rear-view mirror and worry lines creased her brow. Her lips tightened as she flipped on her blinker and moved into the right lane. The truck followed us into the lane, still just a few feet behind them. "What is this a-hole doing?"

You fuckers went too far messing with my wife. Whatever game these guys were playing had gone too far. "Pull into the parking lot up here."

"John, you're not going to get into a fight with a

couple of drunks to start the weekend."

High beams flooded the car. "Just pull in. I'll talk to them calmly. Then they'll go find someone else to bother and we'll start enjoying ourselves."

* * *

Rachel slowed down and turned into the parking lot. I saw a stationary police car there and pointed it out to her. The truck whipped around us and sped off into the night. Rachel found a spot right at the back and pulled in.

She exhaled. "Idiots. Let's get back on the road. The quicker we get to the cabin, the quicker *I'll* relax."

I stared at the road long after the truck was out of sight. "I think we should tell the police anyway. Those guys have been following us for a while."

Rachel returned my gaze with a frown. *She thinks I'm crazy.*

"What do you mean, they've been following us?"

I told her the truck had been behind us earlier and that seeing it in the parking lot of the Sundae School is what had triggered my panic attack. "And obviously,

21

they followed us from there."

Rachel shook her head. "I think your imagination is getting the best of you. Why would they be following us? And if they were, why did they stop?"

I shrugged. "Maybe they saw the police car. Who knows, they're probably just a couple of drunks looking for trouble." *Please let that be all this is.*

Rachel sensed something. "I guess it wouldn't hurt to tell the police. Might save an accident later if they can find the truck before those clowns hurt someone."

She pulled the car over to where the cruiser was parked, and I got out. I approached the driver's side of the car. "Excuse me, Officer?"

The cop looked bored. He gave me the once-over. "What can I do for you, sir?"

I hesitated. What did I *really* have to tell him other than I'd seen the same truck a couple of times? "Well, it's probably nothing, but there's a couple of guys in a pick-up truck that have been sort of harassing us. Tailgating, flicking their high beams, that sort of thing. I think they've been drinking."

The cop got out of the vehicle. He was huge. Taller than me and much broader. His uniform stretched tightly across his muscled chest and arms. He pulled out a notebook, his face a mask of intensity, making him appear a lot older than I'd originally thought. "What makes you think these guys were drinking?"

"Well, it's…they were driving recklessly. And they were yelling out the window at other drivers."

The cop took notes. "Did you get the license plate, or make and model of the truck?"

I slapped my palm to my forehead. "God, I'm so stupid. I didn't think to get the plate number, but the truck is all jacked up and painted black. The windows are tinted really dark, probably illegally." *Might as well pile on.* "Oh, I almost forgot, the word 'badass' is painted on the passenger door."

The cop looked up. His face held an expression I couldn't read. *Does he know the truck?*

"Can I have your name, please?"

I stared at him. *Why?* The cop looked up, waiting for an answer. "Why do you need my name? I'm reporting something proactively here, trying to help."

The cop was annoyed, but forced a smile. "I need your name and contact information in case anything comes from this and I need you to file a report or identify the truck."

I felt stupid for being paranoid and pissing off the cop. "Of course, sorry. My name is John Baxter."

The cop's head jerked up and his eyes narrowed. I took a step back.

"Is something wrong, Officer?"

The cop smiled, but it looked…wrong. "Nothing at all. I knew a John Baxter back in college, just weird to hear the name. And your local address while you're in town?" I almost hesitated again, but gave the officer the information. "Thank you, sir. We'll be on the lookout."

"Thank you. Like I said: it's probably nothing. Have a good night."

The cop tipped his cap and I walked back to my car. I told Rachel about our conversation as she pulled away. The cop never took his eyes off us.

CHAPTER THREE

The rest of the drive to the cabin was uneventful, though I kept turning to look behind us for the truck. After we were off the main road, I had finally calmed down. The number of twists and turns we'd taken through the mountain would be impossible to guess unless someone was right behind us, and I'd made sure nobody was.

I had found the rental cabin by accident. It was right after another fight. I'd been reading the paper; Rachel was in the kitchen slamming shit around. The ad for vacation rentals in New Hampshire stared at me. *Maybe it's a sign.* I looked through the rental pages, eliminating crowded resorts and hotels. *It has to be just right.* I stumbled on the cabin in the mountains, the ad so small I almost overlooked it. It met all my criteria. It was secluded, literally sitting by itself, surrounded by miles of forest with no neighboring properties. No cable TV, not even a phone. The owner considered those negatives, which helped make the cabin afford-able.

The last piece of the puzzle was a romantic set-ting. I wanted everything to be just right so I could try to win my wife back from wherever she'd gone after we lost the baby. The cabin boasted a huge fieldstone fireplace where I pictured us cuddled up in front of a roaring fire. *When was the last time we'd had sex?* I could-n't remember. The cabin also had an enormous deck with a four-person hot tub. It was perfect.

"Can you make sure we're going the right way? I don't know if these roads are even on the map."

Rachel's voice brought me back. I pulled the map out of the glove box and turned on the dome light. "What was the last street sign you noticed?"

Rachel's brow furrowed and I smiled. She was so animated that even the act of thinking was a one-act drama that only I got to see. She blew a piece of hair out of her eyes. *God, she's beautiful.*

"We turned off Stray Brook Road onto Mason's Pass."

I smiled again. "We're almost there."

"Are you serious?"

I nodded. "Mason is the guy who built the cabin, named the road after himself, too. He owns a shitload of this land. Made a bunch of money a few years ago when IBM or GE or one of those big companies bought his little company."

Rachel slowed to round a curve, and three or four deer looked up from their grazing and darted into the forest.

"He retired and built the cabin, but never moved in. Turns out country living and nature and all that weren't his thing. Anyway, his accountant said he should sell it. I guess his fortune isn't lasting the way he thought it would. He mentioned a few trips to Vegas and Amsterdam that I think had something to do with that."

Rachel turned to me with a smirk, then quickly turned back to the road. "Did this guy send you his biography?"

I chuckled. "No, but he gave me the verbal equivalent. I couldn't get him off the phone. He's a guy with a lot of money—at least he *had* a lot of money—but he sounded lonely. I guess he's renting the place out as much as he can until it sells."

Just as I finished, Rachel rounded a turn and there was the cabin in front of us. *Cabin* was a misnomer; even in the darkness the structure loomed large. The headlights reflected off countless windows. Trees surrounded the house, encroaching on it as if Mother Nature wanted to take back what was hers. We pulled up to the end of the driveway and Rachel shut off the engine. Crickets and peepers played background to the owls and occasional coyotes. I inhaled, drinking in the clean mountain air that was redolent with pine and some sort of wild flower that Rachel would probably be able to name. "Let's get the stuff inside and relax." I filled my lungs with the sweet fresh air, then went to the trunk to fetch the bags.

Another sound began to rise over the forest's symphony. I stopped and turned to face the direction of the road. It sounded like a car engine, but I could see no headlights. *You know it sounds more like a truck engine. Maybe a black pick-up truck?* I pushed the thought aside as my heart began to pound. I scanned the darkness for any sign of a vehicle. The woods went quiet, and I strained to pick up the sound of the engine, but could no longer make it out.

❋ ❋ ❋

"Coming?" Rachel was standing on the porch. "Or are you looking for Bigfoot?"

Her playful smile helped calm me. I debated asking if she had heard an engine, but didn't want to ruin the mood. *It was your paranoia; they couldn't have followed us here.* My anxiety could play tricks on me. I wiped my mouth and grabbed the bags, joining Rachel on the porch. I unlocked the front door and let Rachel step in. She found the light switch, and we both gasped when we got our first look at the place.

The pictures didn't do it justice. It was hard to call the place a cabin, considering it was bigger than our house. The front foyer was a mosaic of colors, the tiles probably imported. The rest of the first floor was a huge open floor plan. To the right was a living room with the fieldstone fireplace surrounded by over-stuffed couches and chairs. Beyond that, the walls were lined with bookshelves. To the left was a dining room with an impossibly long oak table that had to seat at least twenty people. The back of the first level was the kitchen, boasting granite countertops and gleaming stainless steel appliances. A spiral staircase of polished wood twirled upwards in the middle of the cabin, where an elaborate chandelier that seemed to be made of some sort of antlers hung. A wooden railing ran around the top of the staircase with all the second-story rooms surrounding it.

"This place is amazing," Rachel said.

"It really is. I mean, it looked great in the pic-tures, but…" I dropped the bags at the foot of the stairs and continued slowly across the room. When I reached the sliders at the back wall, I found a bank of light switches and flipped them all on. The deck lit up like something out of a fairy tale. Muted white lights were somehow embedded in the railing that surrounded the deck. The sunken hot tub had underwater lighting that glowed green. A gas-powered chimenea flickered silently. It was stunning. "Honey, come look at this."

Rachel approached from behind. "Whoa. Let's get out there." She reached for the slider, but I stopped her.

"I have a better idea. Let's bring the bags upstairs, get our bathing suits on, and really check it out."

Rachel gave me a look I hadn't seen in a long time. "I have an even better idea." She peeled off her t-shirt, then reached down to unsnap her shorts. "Let's forget the suits."

In the weeks leading up to the weekend, I had imagined all sorts of marriage-saving fantasies. This beat them all.

I was ripping my clothes off before she finished the sentence. She was already opening the slider and stepping onto the deck. I watched the sleek curves of her body, the way she moved so gracefully, her natural beauty. She slipped into the tub. I went to her.

Rachel was leaning back in the tub with her eyes closed. I reached for her. It had been so long since we'd been intimate that I felt like a teenager. Her eyes fluttered open as if she'd been asleep, and a seductive smile lit up her face. Then all the lights went out. The

31

darkness was so sudden and profound that I wondered for a second if I'd been struck blind. I blinked a few times and my eyes began to adjust. "Rachel…did you do that?" Even the lights in the house were off. The growl of an engine cut the night. It grew louder, and I saw random flashes of light, headlights, bouncing as a vehicle approached rapidly.

* * *

"John…"

Rachel's voice shook. I heard splashing as she got out of the tub.

I jumped out of the tub and stumbled across the deck to the sliders, dressing quickly as the roar of the engine grew closer. My heart was pounding and I was shaking, fear and adrenaline mixing a cocktail that threatened to paralyze me. Rachel was next to me getting dressed.

"John, what's going on?"

I took a deep breath before trying to answer. "I think it's those guys in the pick-up." Saying it out loud made it real. No longer just the product of my overactive imagination or paranoia.

"Why…what do they want?"

I hoped her voice sounded that way from the cool night air on her wet skin. Rachel was fearless, always had been. She never backed down from anything. Whether it was the loss of our child or my drunken tirades that had followed, she always stayed strong.

"I don't know." I wanted to tell her it was just a couple of drunks trying to scare the out-of-towners. *They mean to do more than just scare us.* "Call the police, just in case. I'll go talk to them."

Rachel grabbed my arm. "There's no phone…"

I leveled my breathing and took my wife's hand in mine. "I…I'll talk to them. Reason with them. It'll be fine." Somehow, despite the terror that threatened to cripple me, I drew strength from Rachel's fear. I released her hand and headed for the front of the cabin as the truck approached. It was like letting go of a lifeline in a churning sea. *I'm alone up here. It's up to me to fix this.*

I opened the front door just as the truck turned the corner of the driveway. Its high beams blinded me as I stepped onto the porch. The truck went past my car and pulled to a stop twenty yards away from the porch. The engine idled. I stood my ground, waiting for them to get out of the truck. *They're laughing at me.* I couldn't see into the truck. I remembered the tinted windows and knew it was futile to even try.

"What do you want?" My voice may have been drowned by the truck's engine, but I was sure the men would see me yelling at them and say something.

"John…"

I turned to see Rachel in the doorway. "Get back inside," I hissed.

The truck roared as the driver gunned the engine. Rachel closed the door, and I turned back to face the truck. I threw my arms up. *What the fuck!*

The engine revved again. The truck backed up slowly. It reached the curve of the driveway, turned around, and sped off into the night. I exhaled, all the stress of the last few moments catching up to me. Rachel opened the door and ran into my arms. I held her, my own tremors melting into hers. "They're gone. Just a couple of guys trying to prove they've got balls." *But they'll be back.*

Rachel pulled away, but kept her hands on my shoulders. "Let's get the bags and just find a hotel in town. We can talk to the police again in the morning. I don't want to stay here tonight, okay?"

I sighed. The cabin was perfect, but the reality was I didn't want to stay either. I knew they would be back. Maybe next time they wouldn't leave without whatever it was they wanted. "I think you're right. I'll get the bags. Will you just make sure we closed the sliders?"

I grabbed the bags from the foot of the stairs and headed for the car. As I approached the vehicle, something seemed off. *Maybe it's just the darkness playing tricks on me.* But when I got closer, I knew it was no trick of the light. It was much worse.

The car was sitting at an angle, and I could see the flat rear tire. "Shit." I dropped the bags and went to the trunk. I knew the spare was good. Changing the tire would only delay our escape by a few minutes. I opened the trunk, stopping when I noticed the tilt of the car. Dread gripped me as I moved to the driver's side and saw that tire was flat as well. This wasn't just bad luck; the tires had been slashed. The ball in the pit of my stomach grew. I fished around the glove box and found a flashlight. Both tires were shredded.

The cabin door slammed. Panic took hold when the reality of our situation played out in my head. We had no way to contact anyone and no transportation. It was either hunker down until morning or start walking. I knew those guys would be back. *If Rachel and I stayed in the cabin, would they try to get in? Or would they just make noise and scare us?* I struggled to draw a breath when I pictured the two guys—*were there only two?*—breaking down the cabin door. *Would they beat me up and rape my wife? Would they go so far as murder?* I had to protect Rachel.

"Get back in the cabin. We've got a problem." My voice came out too high-pitched, almost whistle-like.

"John, what is it, what's..." Her eyes darted to the car. "Oh God."

In the distance, the sound of the engine was growing louder again. "Go!" I grabbed the bags and followed her back in the cabin.

CHAPTER FOUR

"John, what do they want?"

I knew what they wanted. And I knew they'd left just so I would have time to see the tires and realize we were trapped. The fear in Rachel's voice threatened to send me over the edge into an abyss of panic. Somehow, I held it together. *For the moment.* "Lock the door behind me."

I threw the bags to the side and searched the cabin with the flashlight from the glove compartment. The open floor plan and walls of windows that a few moments ago were beautiful now served as harsh reminders to our vulnerability. Locks be damned, one rock was all it would take to gain entry. "Rach, come on, upstairs." I pushed her ahead, following just as the twin high beams from the truck splashed through the front windows. "Hurry!"

We reached the top of the stairs. A short hallway led in each direction, with a door on either side. "You go that way; I'll take the other. We're looking for the best place to hole up. Got it?"

Rachel's eyes were wide with terror. I handed her the flashlight before heading in the opposite direction. Outside, the constant rumbling of the truck's engine taunted me. I threw open the first door. A huge bedroom, its two exterior walls were all windows. It was like being in a fishbowl. There was a small bathroom, but the door to it would offer little resistance. Then we would be trapped in *that* small space. My breath shortened to gasps at the thought of it.

I spun and ran across the hall to the other room. It was a mirror image, offering no salvation. Rachel's cry cut through me, and I bolted past the stairs to the other side of the hall. Rachel stood at the window staring down. I strode across the room and stopped next to her as my last vestige of hope slipped away.

The truck was running, high beams still on. Four figures—not two—stood in the harsh glare of the headlights. Two of them held rifles. They were talking, unaware they were being watched. They seemed to be planning to surround the cabin. One gestured wildly, and the others moved in a semicircle around him. *He's the leader, he's the one I need to take out first.* It looked like they were arguing. Finally, the one that had started it held up his hands. They split up and moved towards the house in pairs. Rachel's sobs startled me back to action.

"Let's go." I turned, but sensed Rachel wasn't following me. I went back and took her by the shoulders. Her eyes were hollow, empty of the spark I was used to seeing. "Rachel, listen to me. We have to go. Now."

Her eyes moved toward mine, then back to the scene outside, where the four figures were spreading out. I touched a hand to her cheek and forced her to look away, to look at me. "Rachel, we have to go." Something flickered in her eyes, some sense of recognition. She nodded. I took her hand and pulled her toward the stairs.

"I didn't see any signs of a furnace or a breaker

box on the first floor. That means there must be a basement. Maybe we can hold them off. Or find something…"

We reached the bottom of the stairs, and I fumbled to turn off my flashlight. Two dark shapes were on the back deck, waving flashlights of their own around. I stayed frozen in place, waiting for a sign that they had spotted me. The flashlight beams outside continued to scan the deck. *They're looking for a hidden key. But if they don't find it, they're coming in anyway.* All that mattered was they hadn't seen me and Rachel. Yet.

I surveyed the first floor, searching the darkness for the door to the basement. I spotted a small pantry tucked in the corner of the kitchen. It was the only place I could see that might hide a door. It was also just a few feet and a pane of glass away from the two men on the deck. I took Rachel's arm and motioned for her to get down. *If we stay low, they won't see us. We can do this.*

I went first, army-crawling. My eyes darted back and forth from the windows leading to the deck, back to Rachel, to make sure she was following.

I reached the kitchen and slid across the tile floor,

motioning for her to get ahead of me. She pulled herself into the pantry, out of the line of sight from the deck. I followed. We stood in the pantry, and there was the door, just as I'd hoped. I slid the small deadbolt and pulled the door open. A cool, earthy smell rose from the depths of the darkness. There was something else, something less pleasant in that waft of air that I couldn't identify.

I nudged Rachel, and she felt her way down the first couple of steps. She was swallowed whole by the darkness, then I followed. Once on the top step, I pulled the door shut behind me. For a moment, it was like being sealed in a tomb, the darkness so complete and the earthy odor so strong. It was like being buried alive. I shuddered in the darkness and pushed the thought from my mind.

I flipped the flashlight on, blinking in the sudden brightness. The stairway was steep and narrow. It turned near the bottom, offering me no hint of what lay beyond. My wife moved stiffly, careful not to stumble. She reached the landing and turned, waiting for me to catch up and give her some light. I handed the flashlight to her, giving a quick glance back up the stairs as if there might be someone following. The perspective and the odd lighting were disorienting, making the door we had come through seem much further away than it should be. I shivered, suddenly aware that I did not want to see what was around the corner.

"Rachel…"

She turned the corner. I waited, afraid to follow. I counted my heartbeats, unable to move. *You're a coward, John.* It took me a moment to understand the next sound I heard. It was so foreign, so crushing, that I just stood there, head cocked. It was Rachel. She was… moaning. *Help her!*

I broke my paralysis and turned the corner. At first, all I could see was my wife, shoulders slumped, arms hanging by her side, swinging slowly and causing crazy shadows to dance around her. I stepped behind her and gently moved her to the side, taking the flashlight to see what had broken her. The smell was stronger, part chemical, but still, something else underlying.

The flashlight barely cut a swath through the darkness, as if the dark in this room were thicker, stronger. The floor of the basement was dirt, the room large and open, the walls stone. I panned the light to one side and saw the usual suspects: furnace, hot water heater, and a workbench with some odd-looking tools scattered on it. When I turned the light to the opposite side of the room, I understood. Built into one corner was a prison cell.

* * *

I felt like I'd been gut-punched. My mouth opened wide, trying to get air into my lungs. A fish out of water. The room tilted, and I knew I was on the verge of passing out. Rachel brought me back from the edge. Her plaintive moans could not be ignored. *How could I surrender to unconsciousness and leave her alone, so afraid?* I fought my own panic, shouting down the inner voices and forcing my breathing to slow down. It worked, but it did nothing to reduce the sense of help-lessness I felt. I'd led my wife right where those bas-tards wanted her.

I put an arm around Rachel, raised the flashlight, and began shuffling around the perimeter of the room, easing her with me. There was a door that probably led to a bulkhead. It had a heavy deadbolt on it, at least keeping the intruders from entering that way. If we had to, we could get out that way. *But you know there's someone waiting for you out there, Johnny.* I moved slowly, being careful to be gentle with Rachel. She was in shock, of that I had no doubt. An ugly part of me realized how hard it would be to make a break for it with her as dead weight. I hated myself for the thought.

We inched around the perimeter of the room. I didn't know what I thought I was going to find, but our movements kept my mind focused on something other than my own shallow breathing and pounding heart. There were no sounds coming from above, and I wondered if the basement had been soundproofed from the rest of the house. I passed the cell as quickly as I could, shielding Rachel from it in case she was processing anything. I stopped abruptly. There was a hole in the floor.

I pointed the light down, realizing the strange smell originated from its depths. The hole looked like it had been drilled through rock a few feet down, but that was all I could see. *Did they ever build wells inside?* I gave the hole a wide berth and came to an old metal cabinet. The doors opened with a squeal. The beam fell on a few red cans. and the smell of gasoline wafted up, a pleasant relief from the other odors. I moved the beam down and sucked in a breath. I knew immediately what those other smells were and what the hole was for. *Oh shit, we're in it deep.*

I continued around the room on shaky legs, a feeling of crushing despair weighing heavily on me. Against one wall was a wood stove, its pipe snaking up the wall and eventually through it, presumably to the outside. We arrived back where we started, at the staircase, when I noticed something. I hadn't noticed it before because I hadn't looked behind me.

There was a small door on the wall that closed in the staircase. It was probably just storage space, but I had an idea. I could open the door to the bulkhead, then we could hole up under the stairs. The guys would start searching the woods, thinking we got out. *It could work.* I left Rachel at the bottom of the stairs and moved toward the door. It was oddly shaped to fit the angle of the staircase, making it look like something out of a fairy tale. There was a deadbolt securing it. I slid the bolt and slowly opened the door. I raised my light and almost gasped, a smile creeping across my face. Built into the stone wall was another door, this one made of rough-hewn wood…an exterior door.

Another deadbolt, this one was comically large, like something you might see in a medieval dungeon movie. I tried to slide it open, but it wouldn't budge. I put the flashlight in my pocket and used two hands, grunting with effort. A horrible screech of metal shattered the quiet as the bolt gave way. I yanked open the door, and the cool night air on my face was like a miracle.

My light barely made a dent in the unyielding darkness. All I could make out was the dirt floor and rough stone walls of the tunnel. But the fresh air was all I needed, and I would do whatever it took to reach it. I moved quickly, certain that now we had an escape route, the cellar door above would bang open and heavy footsteps would pound down the steps. I grabbed Rachel's arm and urged her toward the door. Once I had her in the tunnel, I went back and closed both doors, hopeful that they wouldn't find them. *They know this place, John, this is a trap.* I shook off the thought and moved the light around the tunnel side of the door. There was no bolt and nothing to secure it with. *Time to move.* I took my wife's arm and began walking.

"Rachel, we're going to be okay. Stay with me. Come one, Rach, talk to me." I tried a few times to get a response, but when I put the light directly on her face, she didn't even blink. *She'll be fine, once we get out of this.* It was beginning to sound like a lie. I occasionally moved the light back and forth to the walls and up to the ceiling, but there was nothing to see. Dirt floor below, stone walls on either side, a stone ceiling above, and the impregnable blackness ahead.

My mind wandered as we made our way through the dark. Thoughts and memories collided in my head, a confusing slideshow of images. I pictured the tunnel as a birthing tube, our dead baby sliding out. Flash to Rachel, relaying the doctor's message tearfully: there was nothing they could have done; these things happen early on in pregnancies. Flash to me, stumbling home drunk to find Rachel crying, my barely-comprehensible words cutting a wider breach in our marriage. Then me, sitting at the bar, barely conscious, my drunken come-ons to women finally getting me thrown unceremoniously to the curb. Next, me and Rachel in therapy: I don't know how to love a woman who blames me for killing her child.

Flash to me, drunk again, holding a bottle of tranquilizers my doctor prescribed; I throw the bottle aside, too much of a coward to take the pills. Then, me and Rachel sitting side by side on our bed, her suitcases half-packed behind us; "Losing a child is bad enough," she says, "but I won't sit by and watch my husband wrap his own umbilical cord around his neck." Next, me in therapy, alone: "I want my wife back," I say, sobbing. "*I want my life back.*"

The tunnel eventually took a sharp curve, and when we rounded the corner, I realized there was something up ahead. Not something tangible, but just a lighter shade of dark. It was the opening. Tears welled in my eyes, and I recognized that until that very moment, I hadn't truly believed we were going to escape. I quickened my pace, still careful I wasn't going too fast for my wife. "We're almost out of this shit, Rachel. I told you we'd be okay."

When it occurred to me that I had no idea where the tunnel had led us, I turned off the light and slowed down. Better to be cautious in case the tunnel had somehow looped us around to where we might be seen or heard from the cabin. With the light off, my eyes adjusted, and I could see the tree-line, and stars twinkling in the sky beyond. I wiped my lips with a sweaty palm, anxious to be out of the confines of the tunnel. I didn't care if I had to walk all night back to town.

A memory popped into my head and threatened to pull me back into the spiral of fear I had scratched my way out of. It was Quint's story from the movie *Jaws* about being in the water after the *USS Indianapolis* went down. I couldn't remember the exact quote, but it had to do with him being at his most frightened after the rescuers came and he was waiting his turn. *What if after all this…*I shook my head and grunted in frustration. *Why am I sabotaging this?* I slowed the pace even more as we approached the mouth of the tunnel. Part of me wanted to run toward the trees, whooping with joy. The other part was sure we were going to walk right into the four guys holding guns.

I pictured the scene in vivid, heart-pounding technicolor. Four men, two or three of them sporting scraggly lumberjack beards, drinking Budweiser out of cans while waiting for me and Rachel to walk into their trap. They would be wearing jeans and work boots and Harley Davidson t-shirts. They would have guns and knives, and they would start with Rachel…

I reached for the wall to support myself, not trusting my wobbly legs to do the job. Sweat soaked my shirt despite the cool night air, and my heart was indeed pounding. The familiar tingling began in my face and hands, signaling a full-blown, crippling panic attack. I tried to slow my breathing, tried to think of anything but those four men, but it was a losing battle.

"John…"

For a moment, I thought it was my panic playing tricks with my mind.

"Deep breaths, fill the diaphragm, make your belly stick out."

My breath hitched with a sob. *She's back!* Through my tears, I did as she said, breathing deeply, half sobbing and half laughing with joy. When I was sure my shaking legs wouldn't betray me, I stood and pulled her into a fierce hug. "Don't ever leave me." When I felt her arms snake around my waist, I wept.

"Well, ain't that just the cutest."

* * *

A blinding light prevented me from seeing the person who spoke, but I didn't have to. It was one of them. But...*it sounds like a woman?* Still, my worst fears had come true. I tried to shade my eyes, but it was no use; the high-powered beam left everything else in darkness. Finally, the light was lowered to the ground, and I blinked to adjust my eyes, pulling Rachel closer to me.

It *was* a woman. She was wearing jeans and a t-shirt, with her hair pulled back in a ponytail under a baseball cap. She must have seen the shock and confusion on my face. "What are you gawking at?"

"I... Who..." I was flustered.

"Are you with those psychopaths?" Rachel demanded.

The woman smirked, and I saw a hint of something on her face. Regret maybe, or something worse. Humiliation? "Not anymore. Do you want to exchange life stories or get the hell out of here?"

It crossed my mind that this could be a trick to get us to follow, but it didn't make sense. They had the numbers, and more importantly, the guns. They didn't need trickery. "Lead the way," I said.

She crouched low, then headed for the tree line, glancing to the left. *The cabin must be that way.* She reached the trees and signaled for us to follow. I grabbed my wife's hand. "Stay low, just like her." Rachel nodded, and we darted for the trees. I turned my head to the left, and sure enough, spotted the lights of the pick-up in the distance. I was surprised how far we had come underground.

Just before I reached the trees, something caught my eye. At first, I thought it was just a strange reflection from one of the guys' flashlights, but then I saw it again. I couldn't believe it. I stood up to make sure, despite the urgent whispers from the others. "I don't believe it…" A police car was moving up the driveway toward the pick-up truck, blue lights flashing.

"Rachel," I realized I didn't know the other woman's name, "come on out, it's okay." I motioned for them to join me.

Rachel appeared by my side, and I heard her whisper, "Thank God," as she put an arm around my waist. I turned to the other woman, who did not look as thrilled as I was to see the police.

"Hey, what's your name?"

She looked at me for a long second, her face clouded with apprehension. "My name is Elizabeth Brown. Most people call me Liz." She had a faraway look in her eye. Like she was thinking of a better time, a better place. "My smart friends call me 'the poet'."

I smiled. The woman seemed to have a conscience and be reasonably normal. How did she end up with a bunch of gun-toting lunatics?

"Come on, Poet, we'll make sure the police know you tried to help. It's going to be okay."

Liz met my eyes with a half-smile and a look of gratitude. Rachel nodded. "Come on, Liz, John's right. Even if the police hadn't shown up, you were trying to save us. It's no small thing to stand up to a bunch of guys with a mob mentality."

Liz nodded, and we began walking towards the cabin. As we approached, I saw a police officer with his gun drawn. It looked like two of the men were face down on the ground while he was cuffing the third. I wasn't sure whether to call out or not. *Probably better than surprising a cop holding a gun.* "Hello, Officer! My name is John Baxter. My wife and I are renting the cabin."

The cop flashed a powerful light in our direction. I shielded my face, blinded again.

"Get out—"

The words were cut off by something that sounded like a bat hitting a baseball, follow by a grunt.

"Stop right there and put your hands high up over your heads, please. Who's that with you, Mister Baxter?"

I did as the cop asked, making sure Rachel and Liz did as well. The relief I felt earlier was slipping away, revealing the fear that always seemed to be there. *Something isn't right.* "It's my wife, Rachel, and Elizabeth Brown, Officer. She was with these guys, but tried to help us when she saw it getting out of hand."

"That's fine, Mister Baxter. You three come on up, but keep those hands where I can see them until we get this sorted out."

Rachel and Liz started walking. I was letting my anxiety get the better of me again. I walked up the slope towards the driveway. I stopped when I reached the gravel drive, warning bells going off in my head. It looked like the same cop I spoke to earlier, and for some reason, this gave me no comfort.

"Mister Baxter, I'm Officer Locke. We met earlier this evening. I took a spin by to check on things. Looks like a good thing I did."

I nodded. "Can we put our hands down now, Officer Locke?" I stared at the three men on the ground. The guy in cuffs was moaning and squirming a little, but the other two hadn't moved.

"Not just yet, sir. Let me get these three taken care of first. And you say one of the women was a part of this?"

"Yes, Elizabeth Brown was with them originally, but like I said, she came to help us."

"How can you be so sure she wasn't just trying to lure you back here?"

Something in the cop's tone was off. I continued watching the guys on the ground for any movement, any signs of life, but they remained still.

"Officer Locke, I'm Liz Brown." Liz's voice was shaky, but I couldn't be sure if she was afraid of the consequences of being with her three friends or afraid of the cop. "I came up here with them to throw a scare into the weekenders here, but then Bones started talking crazy. He...he did some coke and... I don't know, he was scaring me. We argued, I told him he was pushing it too far, but then he got a look like...I don't know, like he might not mind hurting me either. So, I went along with him and split off as soon as I could."

As Liz was talking, Officer Locke was pulling the cuffed guy to his feet and dragging him towards the cruiser. The urge to bolt was almost overwhelming, but I knew it was just my anxiety. I was being paranoid about the cop. *Why aren't the other two guys moving?*

The man in cuffs was coming to as Locke slammed the door shut. He began yelling, but I couldn't make out what he was saying.

The cop smiled again, and the word that jumped into my mind was *wolfish*. It was a cliché, sure, but it fit. I pictured him wearing that smile as he told Little Red Riding Hood about his big eyes and big teeth. It was a bizarre thought that might have been funny in a different situation.

"All right, let's go inside and figure this out, shall we?" The cop's tone was almost jovial. *Almost.*

I looked at the two men on the ground. The two who had yet to move. "What about them? You can't just leave them there."

Locke stared at me for a long time before answering. "Oh, they'll be fine. They aren't going anywhere." Then there was that smile again.

Rachel started toward the cabin, but I grabbed her arm. "I think I'd be more comfortable doing this at the police station. Maybe you could call for a back-up, or Liz could drive the truck and we'll follow you?"

The cop's smile faltered for a second. Then he sighed deeply and all pretense left his face. He pulled out his gun and pointed it at me. "I guess we're going to do this the hard way. Get in the fucking house or I shoot your wife in the leg. It will hurt a lot, and she'll die slowly from blood loss. It won't be pretty." He moved the gun to point at Rachel's thigh. The wolfish smile returned. *All the better to eat you with, my dear.*

CHAPTER FIVE

I kept Rachel close as we made our way to the cabin, followed by Locke. We passed the two men on the ground, practically having to step over them to get by. That close, I could see the blood pooled around each of their heads. *Christ, he must have slit their throats.* Heat spread from my chest to my face and hands. My fear-stricken brain tried to convince me it was a heart attack, but years of coping argued it was just another panic attack. Ride the wave, my therapist taught me; it eventually crashes and slowly ebbs away.

"Hold on." Locke kept the gun trained on Rachel while he pulled something out of his pocket. He pushed a few buttons and all the lights in the house came on.

The final horrible piece fell into place for me. "You…you're…this is your house."

"Give stuttering John a prize. He cracked the code," Locke said. "Now kindly get your asses in the cabin. I think you can figure out where this party is headed."

My face and hands started tingling, the final step before a paralyzing panic attack. Rachel gripped my hand. "Don't you dare lose it now. Breathe, damn it."

Locke stared at us. This time his grin was genuine. "Are you giving birth?"

Rachel glared at him despite the gun aimed at her.

Liz stepped forward and I saw the seething hatred in her eyes. Her eyes never left the cop's, her voice steady and clear. "It's not enough you're a psychopath, you have to be an asshole, too? Your mother must have done some really weird shit to you when daddy wasn't around."

I barked out a laugh, then waited for the gunshot to destroy Rachel's leg, but it never came. Locke's face twitched. "In the cabin. Down to the playroom."

Liz looked at me. "What does he mean?"

I just shook my head. I flexed my hands a couple of times, relishing the fact that the tingling had subsided. I was feeding off Liz's anger. "It'll be fine, Liz. Let's go."

Locke gave me a bemused look as I passed. I led the way through the house to the kitchen, then down the cellar stairs. Behind me, I heard Liz begin to sob, muttering something I couldn't make out. At the bottom of the steps, I stopped and let Rachel and Liz join me. Liz screamed when she saw the cell and tried to run back up the stairs. I tried to grab her, but missed. She got to the landing and was about to turn the corner when Locke's boot flashed out, catching her in the chest and knocking her backwards. This time I did catch her. She was crying hysterically and gasping for air at the same time.

I helped her regain her balance. "You have to calm down. You have to stay strong."

"*You have to calm down. You have to stay strong,*" Locke repeated, his voice that of a petulant child. A schoolyard bully.

My panic had subsided, giving way to a dangerous rage. I turned to Liz. "I think you were on to something up there. Do you think she made him give her sponge baths? Or maybe she dressed him up like the daughter she always wanted, taping his junk down so he looked more feminine in tights?"

I watched for Locke's reaction out of the corner of my eye. I saw the cop pull his Billy club and take a wild swing at me. I got an arm up to block the blow and managed to grab the club. Then the barrel of the gun was pressed against my forehead, and I pulled my hands away, holding them out by my sides.

"That's strike two, Johnny. Next wisecrack gets your wife thrown down into the hole without the bene-fit of being dead. She'll scream for a long, long time while you and me have our own fun up here. That what you want, Johnny?"

I dropped my gaze to the floor and shook my head. I chewed on the inside of my cheek until I tasted blood. I wanted a drink. The desire for one, the *need* for one, came unbidden. I bit down harder.

"That's what I thought. Now be a good little pris-oner and get in the cell. We've got a lot to do."

❋ ❋ ❋

Locke made us empty our pockets into a basket before we were locked in the cell. It was like being at the airport, going through security, only we wouldn't be getting our stuff back. I considered trying to hold on to my flashlight, or maybe my keys, but in the end, I put everything in the little basket. I was on strike two, after all. I watched with curiosity as Liz emptied her pockets. A few loose bills, a tattered rabbit's foot, and a small plastic bag with what looked like weed. She traveled light. I wondered what goodies her derelict friends would have pulled out of their pockets. If they were alive.

I was doing okay until the cell door slammed shut and the lock clicked home. It hit me: I was a prisoner. And it hit me hard. The tide was coming back in, and it was coming fast. My breath came in shallow gasps, and the familiar tingling in my face and hands began in earnest. I started flexing my hands, terrified that this was going to be a bad one.

At their worst, my panic attacks induced a near-paralysis state. My hands twisted into claws, and I couldn't move them. My jaw tightened to the point I couldn't speak. The first time it happened I was sure I was having a stroke. The doctor at the ER calmly explained there was nothing physically wrong with my brain, but it was an extreme form of anxiety. This began my journey down medication road.

I moved to the back of the cell, mentally running through the times tables. It was something that helped my "self-talk" from taking over and making the attack worse. I saw Locke watching me. He probably thought I was up to something, but his expression changed and he looked on with cruel amusement. Like a kid burning an ant with a magnifying glass.

"Looks like somebody isn't such a jokester now. What's the matter, Johnny? Scared?"

I could block him out; he wasn't the enemy now, I was. *You're going to have an epic panic attack and probably die or go crazy from it.* That was the voice I couldn't block out. Locke was an amateur compared to the power of it. That voice had years of practice tormenting me.

I felt a hand on my arm and tensed. "You need to keep it together, John."

Rachel's voice cut through my panic. It wasn't the same reassuring tone she had in the car. It sounded forced, but it was enough. She kept talking softly while Locke cackled in the background. Once again, as the panic ebbed, the anger returned.

"Johnny, what are the ladies going to say if you piss your pants?"

He was close to the bars, and I lunged at him, reaching through the bars and getting a handful of his shirt. I yanked him towards me. In my mind, I saw his face smashing into the bars, me grabbing the gun and shooting him. Saving us all.

Instead, he grabbed my wrist with one hand and twisted it painfully. Then my wrist was secured to one of the bars with a zip tie. It was tight enough to draw blood. After a minute, my hand began to go numb.

"Strike three, Johnny. I guess I won't need to do eeny-meeny to see who goes first." He ambled over to the workbench and began pushing the tools around. "This should do."

He turned toward me holding a rusty pair of bolt cutters. My heart quickened, this time out of physical terror, not just silly panic. He was going to torture me.

"You're feistier than I thought you'd be, I'll give

you that. I figured you'd be in the corner sucking your thumb by now while I enjoyed all the female wiles your wife has to offer."

He was right in front of me, and I spat in his face. I didn't have much spit, terror will do that. He didn't even flinch, just pulled a hankie out of his pocket and wiped it off. He folded the hankie carefully and placed it back in his pocket.

"Now, where was I? Oh, right. Payment time."

He raised the tip of the bolt cutters towards me. I clenched my hand into a tight fist and began yanking on the zip tie, knowing it was futile. Blood oozed from my wrist. Rachel and Liz were crying while Locke had a gleeful look on his face. In a quick movement, he got the cutters over my pointer-finger knuckle and smashed the handles together. I watched with morbid fascination as my finger dropped to the ground.

CHAPTER SIX

Now

Of course, I didn't tell little Nick what happened. I managed to spin a pretty good yarn involving the deadly combination of power tools and carelessness. No extra charge for the life lesson. All the while I was talking, in my head I was back in that cell, watching my life ooze out of my body by way of my missing finger.

My wife and I never talked about the time we spent in the cell, or how we got out. When Mary came along, it was like a miracle. As she got older and began asking questions about my finger, about mom and dad when we were just married, we invented fairy tales. To little Mary, her parents were like Prince Charming and Sleeping Beauty. It wasn't anything we ever planned, the stories just came out of us like we were telling her the way we wished it'd happened.

"Grampy, how did you meet Nana?"

I almost laughed. Sometimes it was kind of freaky, like that kid was inside my head, listening to my thoughts. I opened my mouth to speak when I realized I hadn't told the story since Mary was a little girl. My wife and I always told the story together, taking turns, filling in little details the other one left out. Now my storytelling partner was in a box and I couldn't do this alone.

I sat there with my mouth open and tears spilling down my cheeks, splashing on little Nicky's head like warm summer rain.

"I think Grampy's had enough of story time, don't you, Nick?" Mary to the rescue.

For some reason, telling my grandson that perfect fairy tale became the most important thing in the world. I *had* to tell it, or I would be tarnishing my wife's memory, our life together. I wiped my face on my sleeve.

"It's okay, Mary. I just might need help on some of the parts…"

My daughter smiled at me and reached over to squeeze my hand. "If you're sure, Dad. It is a great story."

Something about the way she said it sent cold fingers down my spine. *She knew.* "Well, Nick, the day Nana and I met was about as perfect a day as you'll ever see in New England. A sky so clear and blue it made you forget what clouds looked like. The sun shining down on everything like God's smile, and a cool breeze to remind you that there was an ocean nearby."

I watched Mary as I spoke, and she watched me right back. When I faltered, she picked up the pieces of the lie I'd forgotten. Still, in my head I was back in that goddamned cell…

CHAPTER SEVEN

Then

"I was only going to take the pinkie, but you had to go and spit at me." He shook his head like a disappointed parent.

Blood was spilling copiously from my stump. He reached up again with the bolt cutters and severed the zip tie. I pulled my hand in, ripping off my t-shirt to use to staunch the blood flow. Rachel came over to help, raising my hand in the air to try to slow down the bleeding. I looked at Liz and frowned. She was staring at my finger just outside the cell. She wasn't crying any more.

Then she looked up at Locke. I can honestly say I'd never seen a look of such hatred on a woman's face, and I haven't since.

Locke didn't blink. "Don't worry, sweetie, my plans for you don't include cutting off any digits." His expression was a combination of lust and violence that chilled me.

Liz moved slowly to the front of the cell, grasping a bar in each hand. Her eyes smoldered with malice. "I'm going to kill you." She said it in a tone that didn't match the intensity of her gaze, almost matter-of-factly, like she was telling him the time.

Locke looked at her for a second before bursting out in laughter. He had an ugly, condescending laugh that could have been mistaken for a braying donkey. But I watched his eyes and I saw a look I knew well: doubt.

Liz just stared at him, her knuckles going white as she clenched the bars. I don't know what it was about her anger that gave me hope. After all, we were still locked in the cell and I was already down a finger.

Locke stopped laughing and walked up to the cell. I noticed he stopped about three feet shy of the bars, outside of Liz's reach. "Now, I have to go clean up the mess I made outside. Don't you three go anywhere, okay?" With that, he started laughing again and went up the stairs.

Once he was out of earshot, Rachel turned to Liz and me. "We have to get out of here."

The sheer ridiculousness of her obvious statement made me cringe.

Liz didn't seem to notice that Rachel had spoken. "I think maybe Nate and Bones are dead. And…" Her face twitched and she began to sob.

I didn't have the heart to tell her there was no "maybe" about it. "Pete, the one he hit…and threw in the car…he's my brother."

I walked to the far end of the cell. The throbbing mess that was my hand made it hard to think. Something was bothering me, then it hit me, despite the pain. Maybe *because* of the pain. *Why was I alive?* I'd given him more than enough reason to kill me. I thought about the conversation we had when I rented the place. All the questions, seemingly innocent at the time, but now I saw them for what they were. An interview, or maybe an audition. He wanted me alive because we were a couple, Rachel and me. *Had I mentioned marriage trouble?*

The noise from the stairs got my attention. Before he rounded the corner, I already knew he would be dragging one of the bodies down behind him. But I was wrong; he was dragging both. He was a strong sonofabitch, that I learned the hard way, but the ease with which he moved the bodies was frightening, like he was superhuman.

"Hey, listen…"

He turned to me, then went back to the workbench. He came back with an axe. Christ, he was going to hack the bodies up right in front of us.

"Locke!" My yell got his attention and drew curious looks from Rachel and Liz. "The other guy, the one in the car, you don't want to kill him."

He was about to start swinging the axe, but my words gave him pause. He lowered it to his side and looked at me.

"You son of bitch!" Liz screamed and came at me. Rachel grabbed her from behind while I tried to speak to her with just my eyes. It was something Rachel and I were never able to do: communicate without words. We'd just end up looking at each other, con-fused. But Liz seemed to get it, even giving me the slightest nod.

"Go on, Mister Nine-fingers, I'm all ears."

I took a deep breath, and it came out in a sigh. I hoped I was playing it right. "The other guy…" My eyes darted to Liz, then back to Locke. "It's her broth-er." My tone was conspiratorial, like I was sharing a secret with only him.

Locke swung the axe back and forth by his side, contemplating. "Is that so, Miss Liz?"

I watched Liz's lower lip start to quiver and her breathing devolve to short, puffy gasps. "Wh-why do y-you c-care?"

Holy shit, she's playing him. If she had just blurted out a yes, Locke might have thought we were trying to bullshit him. But, this…this brilliant performance of hers, he was buying it without a second thought.

Locke smiled broadly, the sick light in his eyes made me wonder what kind of hell I'd just helped sen-tence Liz's brother to. "I'll tell you what. I'll go see if the young man is up for taking visitors, and we can all have a little chat about it." His eyes narrowed and a fury shone through the slits. "But I promise you this: if you're trying to pull the wool over my eyes, there's gonna be more than just fingers hitting the floor."

He stood there for a long moment, perfectly still. I began to wonder if he was having some kind of mini-stroke or something. An "episode" as the doctors called it when my dad had them. Then his wide smile returned and he looked around at the two bodies. "These guys can wait; I'll be right back." Then he was gone, up the stairs again.

I quickly filled in Rachel and Liz on what I thought was going on. I knew Liz's brother would probably suffer more this way, but selfishly, he was another ally that might somehow get us out of this. At least Locke wouldn't kill him right away.

A few minutes later, Locke returned dragging the third man.

"Pete…" Liz's strangled cry was barely recognizable as a word. Pete's face was a nightmare of swelling and bruises, and his shoulder stuck out awkwardly, impossibly.

"Our friend did not want to cooperate, so I had to show him the error of his inhospitality." Locke lifted him roughly by the handcuff chain, drawing an agonized scream from Pete. He unlocked the cuffs and stepped to the cell. "Now, if you three would kindly step back and make space for your new roommate, the sooner we can commence."

*　*　*

The next couple of hours were some of the worst of that entire nightmare. Locke set to chopping up the bodies of the two men, and he did it with a furious passion. The four of us tried to focus on taking care of my finger and Pete's injuries. We had to pop his dislocated shoulder back in to place. Let me tell you, it's nothing like you see in the movies. It took three or four tries, and I can't even imagine the agony we caused that guy. The time before we finally got it right, he passed out from the pain.

We sat facing the stone wall, our backs to the violence taking place in the room behind us. Unfortunately, there was no way to block out the sounds, and that might have been worse than having to watch. Every time the blade struck flesh or bone, my stomach begged to empty its contents. I don't know how I managed not to throw up.

Then there were the sounds Locke made. The moans and grunts were animalistic, but somehow almost sexual in their pleasure. And he was constantly narrating the action under his breath. *Fucking guy must have drunk his milk; bones are hard as steel. Damn, what the hell did you eat?* I don't know if he realized he was doing it. Finally, it was the sound of the body parts hitting the bottom of the pit with a wet splat. I won't even talk about the smell.

When it was over, Locke went to the cabinet and pulled out a pair of gloves and a couple of sacks of lime. I turned to watch him when I heard the squeal of the cabinet. While searching the cellar the first time, it was those neatly stacked bags of lime that I saw that made me realize just how deep in the shit we were. He ripped a hole in each of the bags and tossed them into the pit. Then he pulled the gloves off and threw them in as well.

"There, that wasn't so bad, was it?" He was covered in gore. Blood, bone chips, and unrecognizable innards clung to nearly every inch of him. "I'm going to go upstairs and take a nice shower. Don't you folks get into any mischief while I'm gone."

Liz left Pete's side and took her place at the bars, veins bulging in her forearms from her grip. She let go with one hand, pointed at Locke with her hand in the shape of a gun, and pulled the trigger. Then she just turned back and sat with Pete. I watched Locke, and even through his mask of blood and guts, I could see fear in his eyes. I smiled and giggled. He turned and stormed up the steps.

Rachel looked at me like I was insane. Maybe I was. "What are you two doing, trying to antagonize him? He just hacked up two bodies and you're— what?—trying to piss him off?"

"Rachel—"

"No, don't. Please, John, unless you want to end up in pieces at the bottom of the pit, just stop."

I stared at her for a minute, but had to look away. Rachel had always been strong in a crisis, but what I saw on her face was resignation. An inability to see beyond the bars, beyond Locke and his madness. Part of me couldn't blame her after what we'd just sat through. But in that moment, I hated her; that's why I looked away, so she wouldn't see my loathing for her written all over my face like a billboard.

Liz stood and walked over to Rachel. "What do you propose we do? Sit around and wait until he lets us go? Is that what you think is going to happen?"

Rachel took a step towards her, closing the already small distance between them. "I'm going to do whatever it takes to get out of here alive. If that means playing nice with the crazy guy, then that's what I'll do." She leaned in even closer. "I suggest you do the same."

"Why don't you bitches just kill each other and save him the trouble." Pete's words came out as a mumbled mess; I think his jaw was broken.

"Pete's right. Knock it off, you two." My words came out bored and smooth, without the edge I'd intended. I had no idea how we could escape with the two women bickering, Pete all busted up, and me...I was just a mess. *A coward.*

"Wait a minute..." Liz went back to Pete. "Pete, he made us empty our pockets. Did he do that to you?"

Pete looked up. I was sure he could only see through one eye; the other was a shiny mess of purple and blue, so swollen the skin looked ready to split. I couldn't even see if there was still an eye in there. "I don't know, I was out." He began to go through his pockets, pulling out a wallet, a pack of cigarettes, a lighter, and a set of keys. Then his eyes—well, his *eye* went wide. He reached under his shirt, and when he pulled out his hand, he was smiling. It was a hideous sight with his fat lips and broken teeth and lopsided jaw, but I had to smile along with him.

In his hand was a leather sheath. He reached with his other hand and slid out the buck knife. With a flick of his wrist, he was holding a glistening, four-inch blade. To me, it looked like freedom.

* * *

Locke came back downstairs a few minutes later, hair still wet from the shower and wearing a pair of jeans and a too-tight t-shirt. He wore his gun belt, too. He was jacked, and he wanted us to know. *The knife will slice the soft tissue in your throat no matter how big your biceps are.* The thought made me smile. I noticed the scars all over his arms and had to bite my tongue. So many nasty "what did mother do to you" comments sprang to mind, but I wanted to keep the peace with Rachel.

"Big arms, little dick. Did mommy use a curling iron to make those marks?" Apparently, Liz didn't care about keeping the peace.

Locke pulled the gun from the holster and moved it between us in a slow arc. "Next word takes the first bullet."

Rachel stepped forward, her hands out in supplication. Looking to keep things calm. "Listen—"

The shot was deafening.

"No!" I jumped forward, but it was too late.

Rachel dropped to the floor with a scream. I ran to her, my hands and eyes searching for the wound. She pulled her hands from her sneaker, and I saw the blood. I got her to lie back on the ground, and I raised her leg and braced her foot against my thigh. I undid her laces and gently pulled off her sneaker and sock.

Her foot was a pulpy mess of shattered bones and bloody flesh. She was rattling off a tirade of swears between agonized moans. I took the t-shirt that was wrapped around my hand and used it to try to slow the bleeding. There was no way her foot would ever be put back together. I looked at the gun, marveling at how much damage a bullet from such a small weapon could do.

I was shocked to see Liz outside the cell with him. While I was tending to Rachel, he must have yanked her out. Pete was up at the bars, screaming at Locke. He turned back at me with a menacing look.

Before Locke came back from his shower, we had put everything back in Pete's pockets in case Locke remembered to search him. Everything but the knife and the lighter—those were in my pocket, but the opportunity to use them had passed. And Liz was going to pay the price.

Locke dragged her over to the workbench. She fought him all the way until he pulled a rag from his pocket and held it over her face. After a few seconds, she stopped struggling and slumped to the ground.

"I like 'em feisty. This one's going to be a lot of fun."

He pulled her up and bent her over the workbench. He took a couple of zip ties from his belt and secured her wrists to a couple of small rings in the stone wall. She was starting to come around, moaning and shaking her head.

Locke stepped back and unbuckled his belt, laying it carefully on the workbench. Then he stripped off his t-shirt and carefully folded it, placing it gently on the workbench as well. His back was a crazed pattern of scars, like a road map to hell.

Pete was going berserk, knowing what was coming. Rachel was in too much pain to care. A desperate thought surfaced of me taking out the knife and throwing it at him, my mind's eye seeing it buried deep in his throat. But I was no circus performer, and it would give away our best chance to escape. I couldn't protect Liz from what was next.

Locke pulled off his loafers and placed them next to the t-shirt. Finally, the jeans came off and he took his time folding them, placing them almost lovingly on top of the t-shirt.

"I'm going to cut your balls off and stuff them down your throat!" Pete was losing his mind with anger and grief, spit flying from his lips as he continued to rant.

Locke turned, and I saw with disgust he was already erect. And Liz couldn't have been more wrong. His penis was huge, almost grotesquely so. He smiled and turned back to Liz. She had regained consciousness and turned her head to see her fate. Her eyes bulged, and she began thrashing wildly. Even from across the room I could see the zip ties shredding her wrists.

I put Rachel's foot down as gently as I could. I grabbed Pete from behind and got him in a full nelson. I dragged him to the far side of the cell and threw him to the floor. It probably wasn't necessary. By that time, he was sobbing, the fight and rage gone, replaced by the scene he would never erase and the helplessness of being unable to stop it.

I held him face down so he wouldn't look. We all suffered through it by way of Liz's screams and Locke's grunts and the occasional slap of flesh. It didn't take long, but it seemed like forever. I was sure for Liz, it *would* be forever.

CHAPTER EIGHT

Locke left her hanging there, slumped over the workbench while he dressed. She was crying in huge gulping sobs that broke my heart. Sometimes the sharp edges of a broken heart cause only pain, sometimes they bring the rage. I was at the bars in Liz's place, the knuckles of my own hands white, fresh blood spilling from the stump where my finger used to be.

Liz was bleeding as well; it was oozing down the backs of her legs and pooling on the ground. It made me realize how insubstantial my missing finger was. What she had lost was so much worse.

Locke cut her down, and I expected her fury to

ignite, but she let him drag her over to the cell by her hair without so much as a struggle. He looked at me and motioned with his head for me to move back. When I didn't, he wrapped Liz's long hair around his hand and yanked. Hard. She screamed, and I moved back. I thought of the knife, but knew it wasn't the right time. Locke was manic, more intense than before. He didn't even bother with her clothes, just threw her in the cell naked and bleeding.

"Can you at least give her back her clothes?"

He didn't even acknowledge me, just jogged up the stairs.

Pete pulled off his shirt and helped his sister put it on. Her sobs had settled into random hiccoughs, and her eyes were swollen from the force of her earlier tears. I looked down at Rachel, but she had passed out.

I had no idea what time it was, but my own exhaustion hit me. The roller coaster of adrenaline and fear and pain and anger is a potent cocktail. I went to the back of the cell and sat, leaning against the unforgiving stone wall. I knew we should be planning, figuring out a way to use the knife on Locke and end this madness, but my mind was shutting down. Between the physical pain of having a finger chopped off and the emotional pain of seeing my wife shot and another woman raped, I was done.

But I wasn't. I tried to let myself fall asleep, telling myself I needed rest to stay sharp, but it wasn't working. In my head, I kept going over the phone call from when I'd rented the place, trying to remember every word, thinking there was a clue in there I was missing that would get us all out of this without the knife.

I was coming up empty, and the frustration was a nightmare paradox: it exhausted me mentally, but pissed me off so that I was too riled to sleep. I kept coming back to my earlier theory about him wanting couples. Not killing Pete seemed to confirm it. But why? So he could rape a woman in front of a man that loved her? I sighed deeply, afraid it might just be as simple and fucked up as that.

I was just starting to doze off when I heard his footsteps coming down the stairs. He had showered and changed clothes again, apparently as bothered by the scent of a woman on his body as he was by having blood and guts splattered all over him. The hatred I had for the man intensified and cleared my head of sleep-fuzz.

He carried a folding metal chair and a notebook. I watched him set the chair up close to the cell—but not too close—and sit down. He opened his notebook and began flipping through the pages. There were a lot of pages covered in writing, and I didn't ever want to know what was written there. Worse, I didn't want to become the subject of whatever lunatic notes he was taking, but in my heart, I knew I was about to become just that.

Rachel was still out. Pete and Liz both had their backs to me, and I couldn't tell if they were awake or not.

"Well, Mister Baxter, it looks like it's just you and I for the moment. Shall we get started?"

I stared at him, trying my best to look disinterested despite the hot anger coursing through me. "Whatever little psycho notes you keep on your victims, I don't want to be a part of. Go back to drawing dicks and balls and leave us alone." I put my head down and closed my eyes.

A second later I heard the scrape of the chair against the floor, followed by his footsteps. I opened my eyes to find him at the bars of the cell, arms folded, watching me.

"I see you are still continuing to struggle to grasp the rules, Mister Baxter. You see, I am quite in charge. You," he laughed quietly, "are not. So, you are welcome to pursue your efforts to be some sort of macho, too-cool-for-school hero and get your pretty little wife in trouble, or you can cooperate. The choice is yours."

I realized the change in him. It wasn't just his clothes—he was now wearing khakis and a loose-fitting polo shirt—but his manner of speaking as well. He sounded more educated, more sophisticated even. And much calmer. Did he take something while he was upstairs, or…? A thought struck me. "I'm sorry. What was your name again?"

He smiled, and I knew. This was not what I knew to be his wolfish grin; this was the benevolent smile of a preacher, or a doctor giving a woman the news her baby was going to be fine. This wasn't Locke anymore.

"Mister Baxter, are you feeling all right? It's Doctor Stevenson. Do you really not remember me?"

*　*　*

For the next thirty minutes, he interviewed me as if I were his patient. His questions ranged from the innocuous to the flat-out insane. What chilled me was how sane he sounded even when asking if I'd ever been abducted by aliens, or if I believed that God existed in the form of a cat.

By the time he was finished—and he wrote everything down furiously in his notebook—the others had stirred. I began to figure out how to use what I knew to my advantage. He had at least two identities; the one who just grilled me, and the one who had…done what he did to Liz. There may be a third in Mr. Mason. I recalled the phone conversation and realized his tone and demeanor then didn't jive with either "Locke" or "Stevenson."

"Doctor Stevenson, why don't you ask my wife how she got shot?"

He looked at me with an unreadable expression. I stared hard, trying to see beyond his eyes, searching for something.

"I think that's an excellent idea. Missus Baxter, shall we begin?"

Rachel looked at me, her face showing a heart-wrenching combination of physical pain and mental exhaustion. I nodded, trying to encourage her, but she just turned away. That unspoken connection still wasn't there.

"Ask me whatever you want." Her voice was flat, devoid of hope.

"Excellent. Why don't you start by telling me about your foot?"

"You shot me." Not an accusation, just a bored fact.

Stevenson wrote in his notebook, turned the page back to review something, then wrote some more. "How did you come to believe such a thing?"

"I started believing it when you pulled the trigger and shot me in the foot. I think I'm done talking. Why don't you ask Pete why he was harassing us? Or Liz how she feels about getting raped by you?"

Stevenson wrote and wrote, his face still neutral.

"You ask me anything, you even look at me, I'll

kill you slower than I planned." Liz was broken emotionally and physically, but she hadn't quit. *Like Rachel had.*

Pete stood up and walked to the bars, one arm hanging limply by his side. "Why don't you come in here where we can have a real conversation?"

"I'm afraid that's against the rules. And as for you Miz Brown, I'd appreciate a little cooperation. Threats are counterproductive in this environment. Let's continue, shall we, Missus Baxter?"

I watched Rachel for a reaction, but she just stared at the ceiling. It pissed me off that she wasn't helping. Pete shuffled back to his spot next to Liz.

"Can you at least get some Advil and water for us? We've all been injured."

He smiled and shook his head. "I'm afraid I'm not that kind of doctor, Mister Baxter."

"Well, whatever kind of doctor you are, why don't you answer this: how did my wife come to have a bullet in her foot when we are all locked in here and none of us have a gun? Quite the locked room mystery, isn't it, *Doctor*?" I spat out the last word like a rotten piece of meat.

Stevenson's face went red, and he stood quickly, tipping over the metal chair. I realized immediately I had gone too far in some way. I didn't think it was the sarcasm; I think it was challenging his delusion. He sighed, folded the chair, and trudged up the stairs like an old man.

"Nice going, John. You probably just got me raped. Or maybe he'll let me off easy and just shoot my other foot off. You could never keep your shit together. At least you have to stay sober in here."

It would have bothered me more if she had said it with some anger, some fire, but all I heard was resignation. Her lack of anger fueled mine. "What do you want me to do, Rachel? Please, I'd love to hear your plan! Do you think he ever lets anybody go? Did you see the pit? Did you see what he did to those bodies?" I stood over her, trembling. I saw red dots appear on her bare legs and thought it was my anger. It was my stump bleeding again.

She just stared at the ceiling.

I paced the cell, my mind a spinning funnel of anger. My pounding heart echoed in my stump as a drumbeat of agony. I looked at my cellmates, searching for hope, but all I saw was a group of beaten and battered souls. Battered both physically and mentally. *Why are they leaving this up to me?*

Liz stood, her face a swollen mess from crying. I forced my gaze to remain on her eyes, not wanting to see her blood-soaked legs and be forced to remember how they got that way.

"John, we need a real plan, okay?"

It was like she'd read my mind. She was the ray of hope I was searching for.

"We need two or three plans, depending on who comes down those stairs."

Liz frowned, and I sensed the others looking at me. Looking *to* me, for answers.

"I think we're dealing with multiple personalities, like that old movie *Sybil*? When he was a cop, he said his name was Locke, but then he became Doctor Stevenson. When I rented this place and spoke to him on the phone, he was Mister Mason."

Rachel snorted. "My husband, the psychologist. Maybe he's just a run-of-the-mill fucking psychopath."

My face burned with rage. I turned to respond, but Pete beat me to the punch. "I think your husband is on to something, let him talk."

She just laughed, all the while staring at the ceiling. "Don't you wish you were still out driving around in your big, penis-substitute pick-up truck harassing innocent people?"

"Who's the psychologist now?" Pete asked her.

"This isn't getting us anywhere," Liz said.

I heard the cellar door open and the footsteps coming down the stairs. Liz, Pete, and I watched. Rachel just stared at nothing.

* * *

He was still Dr. Stevenson. He carried the chair and notebook again, but had a backpack as well. He set up his chair just out of our reach and carefully placed the notebook on it. Then he knelt and unzipped the backpack, pulling out a loaf of bread and what looked like deli meats in plastic bags.

My stomach clenched, not at the site of the food, but in the knowledge that I had to make a move. I sensed his Dr. Stevenson personality was his weakest, his most vulnerable. My hand went to the pocket that held the knife. I glanced at Pete and Liz, hoping they would be ready. They both looked at me, eyes open a bit too wide: they knew.

When Stevenson sat on the chair and opened the notebook, I was disappointed. I wanted this over with.

"I apologize we had to end so abruptly. It occurred to me that you might need sustenance, and I thought we could use that as a...motivating factor for cooperation. A matter of the carrot instead of the stick." He put his head down and began looking for something in his notebook.

He smiled, and I saw a hint of the shark, or the wolf, whatever predator he was when he was chopping up bodies and raping Liz. I gasped when a frightening possibility crossed my mind: what if he was faking?

"Locke, how about some of that food?" I yelled.

He didn't flinch, just kept flipping pages. If he was faking, he was good at it.

"Ah, here we are. Missus Baxter, how long have you been married now?"

I turned to Rachel, desperately urging her to go full bitch on him. Instead, she answered him in a monotone. "Seven years."

My heart broke a little more.

"Interesting," he wrote frantically in his book, "and how many children?"

My entire body went cold. It was as if someone just sucked all the heat out of the room. I began to tremble, just little tremors at first, but escalating into uncontrollable shakes.

"None. No children."

That lifeless voice. So foreign to me, so detestable for some reason. I stumbled to the back of the cell and leaned against the wall, folding my arms against my chest to try to hide my shaking. "Rachel, you don't have to—"

"Please, Mister Baxter!"

He gave me a look of such cunning, so knowing, that I nearly threw up.

"Rachel, certainly a loving and compassionate woman such as yourself wants children?"

I slid down the wall until I was sitting. My legs were shaking so badly they were jackhammering against the dirt floor, drawing looks from Pete and Liz. His switch to using her first name did not escape me.

"I did want children."

I heard a strange noise, like a bark or a hiccough. It took me a second to realize it came from me.

"Past tense? So, you no longer want children?"

I watched him, saw the thirst in his eyes. He'd thrown out his line and hooked a whopper, and he wasn't going to let it go.

"I don't know. It's not that simple."

"Of course it is, Rachel. I mean, you either want to have children someday, or you don't."

His voice was soothing, like he was talking to a child. But his expression was rancid, evil. I had to do something; I knew this would break her. I stood slowly, the trembling subsiding once I started moving. I felt Liz and Pete watching me. I slid my hand into my pocket and felt the cold metal of the knife.

Rachel was still staring at the ceiling, but I saw a tear slide out of her eye and meander down her temple. "You don't understand…" Her words were soft, barely a whisper.

Stevenson stood, his eyes glazed with the thrill of the hunt. He leaned toward the cell. I kept my hand out of sight and unfolded the blade, inching closer.

Pete was standing now, moving closer from the other side of the cell.

"Help me understand, Rachel. That's what I'm here for, to listen and understand. To help people heal."

"I was pregnant once…"

Her words ripped the scab off my heart. The pain of our loss was a fresh wound again, open and bleeding.

Stevenson inched closer. My stomach tightened when I saw his pants bulging. Rage engulfed me like a hot wave. My skin was burning; I could feel my own heat radiating. Pete had moved next to me. His body was helping shield the now-open knife from Stevenson's view. I don't think he would have noticed if I was holding a Samurai sword.

"You were pregnant, but you have no children?" His voice, so calm and sympathetic, but so *hungry*. He was close to the cell now, close enough. I could feel Pete next to me, waiting for me to make my move.

"I…I was pregnant…but I got an abortion…"

Everything stopped. The air was sucked out of the room, and I couldn't draw a breath. *What was she doing? Why was she lying to him now?* Pete was whispering something, but I couldn't make out his words.

"I'm so sorry, Rachel. But why?"

"John…he was drinking…out of control…I couldn't bring a child in to that situation so…"

Stevenson was grinning, his breath coming in shallow gasps. He bent his head to write something in his notebook. I heard a guttural roar and felt the knife ripped from my hand. Pete lunged at the bars, the blade glistening as he thrust it toward Stevenson.

Stevenson looked up just as the knife cleared the bars. His movement was fast, unnaturally fast. He dropped the notebook and grabbed Pete's wrist. He gave it a vicious twist, and I heard bones snap. He grabbed the knife with his other hand while yanking Pete toward him with ferocious strength. Pete's face smashed the bars, and I saw a tooth fly out of his mouth and land in the dirt. I wondered where my finger was. Stevenson brought the blade across his throat without hesitation.

Blood spurted from the gaping slit in Pete's neck. He tried to back away, but Stevenson held him there, pinned against the bars, while Pete's lifeblood showered him. The grin never left his face.

CHAPTER NINE

Now

You see now why my daughter, Mary, was such a miracle? Nick was sound asleep in my lap long before we finished our fairy tale. I didn't notice him conk out. Mary knew he was asleep, but—God bless her—she just kept going. Humoring her old fool of a father. *Or maybe testing me.*

While we were talking, when it was her turn, she changed the story. Just little bits here and there, like she was trying to see if I remembered things or was just making it up. Just like little Nick seemed to be able to see inside my head, his mother could do the same.

Jeff took Nick from me and whispered good night before he carried his son up the stairs. I saw the look he gave Mary before he went, and I dreaded what was to come. She had waited long enough and was going to ask for the real story. I wasn't ready for that. I'd never be ready for that.

As I watched Jeff stagger up the stairs with the extra weight of Nick in his arms, all I could see was Stevenson trudging up the basement steps carrying that folding metal chair.

Mary's eyes were on me; I didn't have to look at her to know it. She was waiting for Jeff to be out of earshot and the question I'd been avoiding since she was born would hit me like a kick in the head.

I took a deep breath and screwed up the courage to meet her gaze. I was shocked to see tears on her face. "Mary, what is it?"

She smiled and wiped her face. "I just love you. You've always been such a great dad. And now you're a great Grampy to Nick…"

"But…" I smiled back at her. I could have made it easy for her. I could have said I knew what she wanted to ask me. There was still a part of me that was hoping I was wrong, hoping for another stay of execution from the truth. From shattering her image of her father.

She cleared her throat and glanced at the stairs. I don't know if she was waiting for Jeff to return, or making sure he wasn't going to. "Dad, that story… I've heard it a million times, and I love it. But…"

I couldn't make her say it. "But you want the truth."

She drew a shaky breath and nodded. "I do."

"Even if it makes you think less of me?" The tears were rolling down my face, but I wouldn't give them the satisfaction of wiping them off.

"I could never think less of you, Dad."

I barked out an ugly excuse for a laugh. "You might want to hold that thought until you hear the real story."

"I mean it." She moved closer and took my hands in her own. "Whatever happened helped make you the person you are. Made you and Mom the great couple you were. Made you both great parents. I've wanted to ask for so long. I've seen the pain in your eyes—Mom's too—every time you had to tell that fable."

I squeezed her hands and nodded. "This isn't going to be easy for me. I doubt it will be any better for you."

She had a look of such intensity that I knew this was it. She wasn't going to back down. I dropped my eyes first and nodded. "Wait here." I stood and went to the back room where my wife used to do her painting. She loved the natural light—something we both craved after what we'd been through. I had a small corner of the room that was a makeshift office. I sat down at the desk and opened one of the file drawers. There, in the back, was my secret, where it had been waiting all these years.

CHAPTER TEN

Then

All of that happened. I *saw* it happen. But all I could hear and see and smell and think about were those four words: *I got an abortion.* And Rachel, she just remained on the floor, staring up at nothing. The last three years of my life were a lie. She stole them from me and didn't have the decency to even look me in the eye. She had confided in a psychotic schizophrenic or split personality or whatever the fuck he was. But not in me.

Nobody said anything. Stevenson, or whoever he was at the time, marched up the stairs and slammed the door. I have no idea how long we all remained silent. The smell of blood and human waste filled the air. Pete's body and clothes were soaked in both.

I finally realized I had nothing to say to Rachel. What do you say to someone that took your unborn child from you? Somehow, I could just put the whole thing away. I took those four words and all the feelings and contemplations that went with them and locked them all in a vault in the far reaches of my mind. There would be time for all that later. Maybe.

All the exhaustion and fear and pain vanished. I became hyperfocused on one thing: killing Mason/Locke/Stevenson and getting out of that cell. Not necessarily in that order. I paced back and forth, stepping over Pete with each lap. Liz said something, but I didn't hear, or couldn't process it. I was rapid-firing ideas in my head and dismissing them just as quickly as they came. The more I paced, the more outlandish the ideas became. It occurred to me that I might be losing my mind, but I discarded that idea along with the rest.

Then Liz was standing in front of me, hands on my shoulders, telling me to stop. I had a nasty moment where I considered throwing her aside so I could continue pacing. Thankfully, I managed to dismiss that idea as well.

"John, please, listen."

Something clicked, or at least brought me back. She was staring at me with a look that was a horrible combination of desperation, fear, and sadness. It balanced my anger somehow, replacing the madness with a new sense of drive. Instead of the random delusional plots of moments ago, I became surgical, calculating. This was a puzzle—and I was good at solving puzzles.

"I'm all right, Liz. I think he's going to be Locke when he comes back down. We have to be ready. *You* have to be ready."

Her face crumpled, folding in on itself when my meaning became clear. I remained clinical, seeing her as just another puzzle piece that needed to be moved to the right place.

"John…"

I reached out and took her face in my hands. "You have to be ready. You have to be strong." Rachel snorted in derision, but I ignored her. "This might be our last chance."

She nodded, tears pouring from her empty eyes. My words had stripped away her humanity. She had become the puzzle piece. I told her my plan.

※　※　※

When the door finally creaked open, I watched in detachment as the cowboy boots appeared, followed by jeans, a gun belt, then a tight silk shirt, and finally Locke. He had showered again; his hair was still wet, slicked back. His face was flushed. He was smiling.

I gripped the bars, ignoring the pain in the stump where my finger used to be. *Had I always been missing a finger?* I couldn't be sure. Liz huddled in the back of the cell, whimpering. Rachel remained on the floor, staring at something only she could see.

"I'm gonna need you to step to the back of the cell, Mister Baxter."

He never looked at me, and when I followed his gaze, I held my breath. Icy sweat broke out on my forehead. The best-laid plans…

"I'm not gonna ask again." His hand moved to the butt of his pistol.

I could only stare; the screaming in my brain made movement, made clear thought, impossible. His hand moved in slow motion, pulling the glistening gun from its holster. A voice rose above the chaos in my head. *You won't be any good to anyone with a bullet in your foot.* My hands released the bars and I stumbled to the back of the cell, not stopping until my back met the rough stone wall.

Locke smiled, and a vision of my hands around his throat—his face purple, tongue lolling uselessly—hit me so hard I matched his smile. His grin slipped. Mine remained.

"Missus Baxter, I'm going to need you to come with me."

I heard Liz gasp, finally figuring out what I already knew. Rachel's head turned slowly to look at him. She stared at him, her expression blank. "I don't think so." Her head turned slowly back toward the ceiling.

Locke's face turned red, and my vision of strangling him returned. His eye twitched, and his hand moved once again to the gun. "I wasn't asking." Clipped words through clenched teeth.

Rachel didn't move.

"If I have to come in there and drag you out, it's not going to go well for you."

Nothing.

He pulled the gun out and reached into his pocket with his other hands and pulled out the keys. My eyes slid to the right, meeting Liz's. Her eyes widened, and I gave an almost imperceptible nod.

Locke lifted the keys to the cell door. I tensed, ready to pounce, telling myself I was ready to risk getting shot. Then Rachel sprang to her feet, letting out a screech when she put weight on her shot foot.

"Fine, let's do this, creep."

Her voice was that of a weary customer service rep bored with her job. I relaxed, relieved and disappointed that Liz and I didn't get our shot. There was no sense charging if he wasn't even in the cell. We would have to wait for another opportunity.

As Rachel stepped out, it hit me what this meant: my wife was about to be raped in front of my eyes. Despite what I now knew—those words that were locked safely away—I couldn't take this.

The blur of movement caught my eye first, then

the gunshot exploded and I jumped to my feet. Rachel had latched onto his gun hand before he could close the cell door. She had his forearm with both hands and all her teeth. They staggered towards the center of the room as Locke grabbed her by the hair and tried to yank her off, but she was holding on like a pit bull.

Liz was up and out of the cell before I had managed to stand. She raked her nails across his face, leaving bloody gashes in their wake. I hoped she would rip his eyes out. With a roar, Locke grabbed Liz by the face and threw her back towards the cell. She stumbled and smashed her head on the bars. The sound was sickening and stopped me in my tracks momentarily. Liz crumpled to the ground, and I watched blood pool around her head before breaking my paralysis and lunging at the door.

Locke had managed to rip Rachel—and a sizable chunk of his forearm—away and threw her aside. His arm was in bad shape. A flap of skin dangled loosely, exposing what looked like raw meat and sinew. Blood gushed as he reached up and slammed the cell shut. I had no idea where the gun was.

I reached the door, screaming in frustration that

Locke had managed to lock it. I lunged through the bars and got a handful of his shirt. He was off-balance, and I managed to yank him towards me. I grabbed his injured arm with my other hand and plunged my thumb into the gaping wound. He screamed in agony, and his knees buckled. I lost my grip on his shirt. He used his good hand to punch me in the balls, and I melted to the cell floor, seeing fireworks everywhere and gasping for breath.

Liz had stirred, and from my vantage point on the ground, I saw her crawling towards the gun. Locke saw her, too, and leapt awkwardly, landing on her back, scrabbling for the gun himself.

A flash of red exploded in my peripheral vision, and I turned as Rachel smashed a gas can on Locke's head. The can was open and gas splashed everywhere, the impact jarring the can from Rachel's hands. Locke's head was split, oozing blood. Gas poured from the can, mixing with Liz's blood from her head wound, the red river oozing through the bars into the cell.

Locke stood, stomping on Liz's hand as she reached for the gun while throwing a vicious punch at Rachel. It connected to the side of her head with a crunch, and she staggered backward as Locke shook his head, sending droplets of gas and blood in a shower around him. He grabbed Liz by the hair and threw her towards the pit. As he bent to retrieve the gun, I reached in my pocket for Pete's lighter.

❋ ❋ ❋

"Rachel, get away!"

Locke's hand was on the gun. Rachel was dazed, but was staggering back toward him. She turned at the sound of my voice. I flicked the lighter and touched it to the sweeping river of blood and gasoline.

WHOMP!

The initial blast of heat threw me backward, the intensity of the flash blinding me. I smelled burning hair and heard screaming. Locke staggered to his feet, completely engulfed in flames. Somehow, he was able to raise the gun and start firing. Then a second, larger explosion ripped through the room. I fell backward again, knowing the gas can had blown. My mind went to the metal cabinet full of other red cans.

I stood and blinked, dazed at the scene before

me. Locke was still standing, a human torch. I watched him burn; his skin was bubbling and sliding off him. His face seemed to change as it melted and blackened. For a second, I thought I saw the three individual personalities flash beneath the flames, right before he fell to the floor.

Beyond the inferno, I saw Rachel on the ground. She was unconscious, but untouched by the flames. Liz was also out of the reach of the gas spill. She was just getting to her feet. She looked dazed and unsteady, too close to the pit for her own good.

"Liz!"

She stepped back from the blaze, careful to avoid the pit. She was at the cabinet and started tossing the gas cans down into it. It was exactly what I was about to tell her to do.

That mental connection again.

"Upstairs, grab something to smother the fire!"

She still didn't look all that steady, but she moved quickly. The room was heating up and filling with smoke. *Burning to death or asphyxiating in this shitty cell is not how I'm going out.*

Liz stumbled back down the steps dragging a comforter behind her. She threw it on top of Locke and stomped on it. I knew she wasn't trying to save him; she wanted the key, same as I did. I searched for any sign of movement from Rachel while Liz battled with Locke's burning corpse. She hadn't moved.

Liz pulled the tattered comforter off the smoldering remains of Locke. She ran back upstairs and came back with a pot of water, dousing his pants. The sizzling stench that erupted is something I couldn't describe. Then she was at the cell with the key, opening the door.

I shoved past her, telling her to get the bulkhead open. I went to Rachel's side and stopped. Her eyes were open, but I knew she was gone. She looked no different than she had when she was in the cell, staring at the ceiling. I knelt next to her. Her left arm was splayed across her chest. When I moved it, I saw the wound just below her breast; the bullet must have been a direct hit to her heart.

A burst of cool air that smelled like pine and earth and heaven stirred the flames behind me. I rose to my feet and turned, staring at the carnage. Locke and Pete were both burned beyond recognition. Liz was next to Pete, using the remnants of the comforter to smother the flames on her brother. She looked like death herself. She looked up at me, then at Rachel, then back at me. I shook my head.

CHAPTER ELEVEN

Now

I waited like a guy on death row as Mary read the articles in the scrapbook. She never had much of a poker face, and I watched the gamut of emotions play out on her face like a silent movie. Shock, anger, sadness, horror, and everything in between. Not once did she look up. *That's a bad sign, and you know it.*

She closed the book. It felt symbolic. I fully expected her to get up and walk away without a word. I wiped the back of my hand across the desert of my lips, something I hadn't done in forever.

"Rachel Mary Baxter was you first wife's name?

You and mom…you named me after her?"

Finally, she looked at me. There were tears in her eyes, but her expression wasn't sad. She looked so much like her mother that it made me dizzy.

"That's right," was all I could manage.

"I don't know what to say."

There it is. "I know, I'm sorry."

"Sorry? For what?" Her hand snaked into mine.

I cleared my throat, not trusting my own voice. I rubbed my ghost finger. "All those terrible things…" I let the words die; they didn't matter.

"Dad, you and Mom, you're heroes."

I thought I misheard her, but when I looked up, I saw the admiration on her face. "I'm no hero, Mary."

"The article said that guy might have been responsible for over twenty deaths. If you hadn't stopped him…how many more?"

I shook my head. The guilt had been a part of me for so long now I wouldn't part with it that easily. "I'm responsible for my wife's death. Don't you see…?"

"No, I don't see. All I see are people thrown into a nightmare and two of the good ones making it out."

I began to argue, but she put a finger to my lips.

"No more, okay?" She put her head on my shoulder.

We sat that way for a long time. I don't know what she was thinking, but I was running through the entire set of events in my head. *What could I have done differently?* I'd been over it a million times and imagined every possible scenario. Confronting the guys in the pick-up sooner? Overpowering Locke before we went into the house? Getting to him sooner, before Pete and Rachel had to die at his hands? But in the end, I couldn't change any of it. In the end, the years Liz and I shared were the best years of my life. Now I had Mary and little Nick.

"When Nick gets a little older, I want him to know the truth."

Her voice startled me; I thought she might have drifted off. Again, I began to protest, but stopped myself. Maybe she was right. Maybe what's left is what's important, not what was left behind or what road you took.

"I think that's a good idea," I said.

"Every kid thinks their grandfather is a hero. Nick's really is." She stood and kissed my forehead. "Goodnight, Dad. I love you."

"Goodnight, kid. And thanks."

"For what?"

I stared at a picture of Liz and me on the end table next to the couch. We were standing on a beach with our backs to the water, laughing. Mary had taken the picture when she was just a kid herself, so we were kind of off-center. Behind us, an enormous wave was about to break over us. Just seconds after the picture was taken, we were knocked over by the wave and came up sputtering and still laughing. We were so happy, blissfully unaware of what loomed behind us.

It struck me that the weekend getaway was just the opposite. We weren't happy to start with, Rachel and I, and the tragedy that hovered over us as we headed to the cabin had no impact on our happiness, or lack of it. My intention was to save my marriage, but it was beyond repair. Those four words she spoke in the cell were just the eulogy; our marriage was dead long before that.

But in that looming wave was Liz, and eventually Mary and Nick.

I stood, suddenly exhausted. "For making your

dad feel like a hero."

ABOUT THE AUTHOR

"Tom Deady is a true storyteller, and I can offer no higher words of praise."

–Richard Chizmar

Tom Deady is the author of *Haven*, winner of the 2016 Bram Stoker Award for Superior Achievement in a First Novel. His second novel, *Eternal Darkness*, was released in early 2017, and his writing journey has just begun. He has a Master's Degree in English and Creative Writing from SNHU. Tom is a lifelong resident of Massachusetts, where he is hard at work on his next novel.

And check out these other novellas from
Grinning Skull Press

Death awaits you. Tim Ritter has just a few months left. At least that's what the doctors have told him.

But then he's been offered a second chance at life – and love. For a price. But is the price too high? The sacrifice too great?

Find out one man's answer to those questions in Dan Foley's *Gypsy*, now available in print and for Kindle, Nook, and Kobo e-readers.

THE DEMON GUARDIAN

Neil Davies

It all started with the sibilant, unintelligible whispering and the movement of shadows within shadows. For Dennis Parkes, it was a sign of his worsening mental health. That is, until the day it spoke clearly and told him what it wanted.

Elsewhere in town, two amateur ghost hunters unearth what is believed to be *Gjallarbru*, a mythological bridge that connects the worlds of the living and the dead.

The dead are looking to cross over, as is the demon guardian, a guardian that has a craving for human flesh. As the veil between worlds weakens and darkness spreads over Ottmor Wood and the surrounding area, it's up to a group of friends to save their town, but are they enough? They have to be—because if they fail, the darkness will continue to spread, devouring everything in its path until there's nothing left to consume.

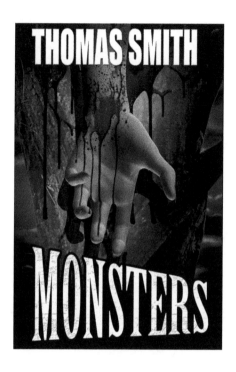

"I killed my parents when I was thirteen years old."

And now, with the murder of Missy Blake twenty-two years later, it's time for Jack Greene to finish what he started.

When the co-ed's mutilated body is found, the police are clueless, but Jack knows what killed the pretty college student; he's been hunting it for years. The hunt has been going on for too long, though, and Jack wants to end it, but he can't do it alone. The local police aren't equipped to handle the monster in their midst, so Jack recruits Major Kelly Langston, and together they set out to rid the world of this murdering creature once and for all.

Lightning Source UK Ltd.
Milton Keynes UK
UKHW020943250820
368797UK00013B/2760

9 781947 227026